INN LOVE

Lighthouse Lovers
Book 4
_____

SHANNON O'CONNOR

Copyright © 2025 Shannon O'Connor
All rights reserved.

All rights reserved. No part of this publication may be reproduced, distributed, or transmitted in any form or by any means, except in the case of brief quotations embodied in critical reviews and articles.

No use of AI was used to create this book, cover or edit any of the following. Please do NOT use my words, cover, or anything from this book in an AI form to feed AI.

Any resemblance to persons alive or dead is purely coincidental.

Cover by PagesandAdventures.

Edited by Victoria Ellis *Cruel Ink Editing & Design*.

Proofread by *Cruel Ink Editing & Design*.

Formatted by Shannon O'Connor.

❀ Created with Vellum

In Love Playlist

I F*cking Love You - Zolita

Sexual Vibe - Stephen Puth

Planet - Aidan Bissett

Like Heaven - Zolita

Call Me Maybe - Carly Rae Jepsen

Cherry Blossom - Joshua Bassett

Cure - Valley

Midnight Sky - Miley Cyrus

LUNCH - Billie Eilish

Adore You - Harry Styles

Worse Things Than Love - Timeflies, Natalie La Rose

Casual - Chappell Roan

Lovefool - Bad Suns

Not My Style - Kate Grahn

ONE

Zara

"The Inn is up on the left." The cab driver points ahead of us, and I squint through my shades and see Harbor Inn—my home for the summer.

"There's not much to do in this town; a lot of the life is in the next town over. But maybe that's what you're looking for. Where did you say you're from again?" I consider lying, my New York instincts kicking in, but then I remember this town is literally called "Lovers." This guy is clearly just trying to be nice.

"I'm from New York City."

"Ah, yeah, definitely not anything like that here. If you miss the city, you should take a ride over the bridge. There are clubs and a big nightlife scene." He goes on and on about it, and I nod politely. I wish there were an option to say, *I'd prefer not to chat on this ride* like the Uber app has.

He pulls up the hill and parks in front of the Inn. The building is smaller than I imagined, but there aren't any hotels in this town, so it'll have to do. The driver helps me with my luggage, and I pay him with a big tip. He was kind, and I can afford to be generous. I head inside, and it's abundantly clear: I'm not in New York anymore.

The interior of this place reminds me of a grandma's home.

Not my grandma, she lives in Vegas with her husband—a husband who is twenty-five years younger than her. She has a penthouse and smokes pot on the weekends. But this place...it has light-colored walls with lace curtains, and the furniture doesn't match. It gives off a major *thrifted* vibe.

Now that I'm here, I'm pretty sure I know why my agent sent me to this town.

I'm on a mission to write a small-town dark romance. Too many big books are set in New York City, and it's becoming repetitive. She wants me to branch out and create a series in a small town. I'm always down for a challenge, and I know that's what this is going to be. There's no way my normal vibes will fit into a place like this. Fuck, I don't even feel like *I* fit into a place like this.

I glance down at my ripped jean shorts, the black crop top that says, *Don't make me cry, I'll come*, which gained me more than a few looks in the airport. Still, it's my vibe and somewhat of a disguise when I travel. I'm not famous by any means, but I am a bestselling author and well-known. I've had my photo taken while traveling way too many times to travel in leggings and a sweatshirt. So I always look photo ready.

I glance around the empty lobby; I'm surprised there's no one here to greet me. I guess they aren't concerned about people breaking in or robberies. I keep reminding myself that I'm not in New York anymore. This is definitely going to take some getting used to. I pull my suitcases up to the front desk and see there's a bell, a literal bell, that says *ring for service*. I do and a voice calls out from around the corner.

"Be right there!"

The voice sounds a bit breathless, so I wait patiently. Then, a woman who has to be my grandma's age comes around the corner. She has short gray hair, a wrinkly face, and a cane covered in stickers.

"Hi, I'm just here to check in." I smile as she walks over to the desk.

"Miss Grey?" she asks, picking up a pair of reading glasses and putting them on.

"Yes."

"I have your room all ready. We don't often get someone staying for such an extended amount of time. I know you requested a room with a view, so we gave you the lighthouse view room. I just need to see a form of ID and your credit card to confirm everything."

"Of course." I fish around in my purse for my wallet and hand her the two cards.

She pokes at the computer crazily slow as she confirms my information. I glance at the photos behind her on the wall. They must be from when this place was first opened. There are two young women, one that looks a lot like the woman in front of me, at a ribbon cutting ceremony in front of Harbor Inn. I wonder who the second woman is. I'm about to ask when I feel something licking my bare toes.

"Oh, hello." I duck down to pet the golden retriever that's licking me. "Who are you?"

"Oh, no. Sorry. That's Sandy. I told her to stay in the back. You aren't allergic, are you?" She looks concerned.

"Nope, I love dogs." I smile as I pet behind Sandy's ears. She wags her tail and licks my knee.

"You do, huh? Maybe I can offer you something? I can take a bit off the price of your stay if you can take her for a walk once each night. My granddaughter comes each morning, but I can't see that well at night, and I haven't found anyone else to do it," she explains.

"Sure, I'd love to." I nod. Sandy seems easy enough, and I feel bad for this old lady. I wonder if she lives up here all by herself. She has to be lonely.

"Lovely! Well, here's your key. You're the only guest currently, but we will have arrivals and departures throughout the summer."

"Sounds great." I take my key and follow her directions to the stairs.

I try not to make a face when I realize I'm on the third floor, and this place has no elevator. I guess I'll be getting my steps in this summer. I'll have a killer ass by the end of my stay.

Thankfully, no one is around to see me huffing and puffing as I reach my room. I set down my luggage and unlock the door. Once inside, I notice the space is huge. There's a queen-sized bed in the middle of the room and a flatscreen TV on the wall across from it. I walk through the carpeted room and find that there's a small step and a second room with a couch, a coffee table, and a desk facing a window. Pulling back the curtains, I pause. The view is phenomenal.

Boats are sailing close by, and the blue waves are crashing along the shore. There are a few people scattered in the water and on the beach nearby, but they're far enough away that they can't see me up here. I'll definitely be able to get some writing done this summer—this view is killer. I can't wait to see what this looks like at night. I'm in awe. I've been in the city for so long; I can't remember the last time I saw an actual beach that wasn't overcrowded with tourists.

I decide to shower before I adventure to town. My shirt doesn't seem appropriate for this climate, and I'm gross from flying out here. The bathroom here is bigger than my living room back home. The bathtub is something I'll for sure be taking advantage of this summer. I scrub off the remnants of the airport and wrap a fluffy white towel around my body. My hair drips down my shoulders as I grab my bag and look for my brush.

Shoot. I just remembered. I need to charge my cell phone. It died during my cab ride, and I haven't even thought about it since then. My mother and best friend will probably be worried about me. They both have my location, but they prefer a text or phone call, so they know I'm safe and sound. Sure enough, once my phone powers up enough to turn on, it blows up with texts.

Before reading any of them, I send out texts to each of them to let them know I'm at the Inn and I'm safe.

Haley instantly calls me.

"I was worried about you! I told you to make sure your phone was charged," she scolds.

"I know, but I took a pot gummy on the plane and knocked out. I swear I'm fine," I assure her. I place her on speaker phone and toss my phone on the bed while I look for clothes to wear.

"How is it? Find your muse yet?" she asks.

Haley thought I'd find my muse on this trip and never get writer's block again. I think it's more wishful thinking, considering she's my best friend and also my editor.

"I doubt I'll meet someone like that *here*." I laugh.

"That bad?"

"No, it's nice. But it's definitely not New York City. It's so *quaint*. It's quiet as hell, and I doubt they have more than one coffee shop in town. I definitely didn't see any Starbucks or Dunkin' on the way."

"Even more reason to stay! Maybe quiet is just what you need."

"For the summer, sure. But I'll be missing the night lights and the noise any minute now."

"Well, I have to go, but make sure you send me pics and remember me when you meet the one."

"Bye, love you."

"Love you, too!"

She hangs up, and I clip my wet hair back. It's hot today, so it'll be dry shortly. I grab my laptop, notebook, and pen and slip everything into my canvas tote. My phone isn't fully charged, but it's good enough to go exploring. I'm sure one of the locals will help me if I can't find my way back here.

Now it's time to go see what this small-town is all about.

TWO

Kim

Harry Styles blasts through my speakers as I dance around my classroom. It's mid-July, and I'm one of the only teachers here setting up my classroom early. I hate waiting until the last minute. The first year I was student teaching, my lead teacher was still decorating her classroom two weeks into the school year. That brought me way too much stress, and I vowed that wouldn't be me. So, when I decided to move back to Lovers, Maine as a kindergarten teacher at Lovers Elementary, I knew I wanted to be done early. Plus, there's no one around to bother me. A lot of the other teachers are on their vacations and want nothing to do with school yet. It's the first year I get to have complete control over the classroom, and I know I need a plan.

I spent the first day cleaning out every inch of the room. I'm sure the other teacher did their best, but I want things to shine—and that meant a bit of elbow grease and that pink cleaning stuff. Then, I decided to decorate the walls and bulletin boards. I have over a thousand ideas pinned on Pinterest, but I know I need to appeal to five-year-olds. So, I found some videos on how to create Bluey-inspired boards. I'm excited about them, and I think the kids will be, too.

I hum along to Harry's songs, and I wonder if the kids even know who he is. I remember seeing a TikTok video about kids not knowing who One Direction is anymore. And let me tell you, that hurt my heart—and made me feel old.

I'm even paying tribute to Bluey on my door by having a *Treat People With Kindness* sign. It's the exact vibe I'm trying to bring into the classroom.

Honestly, it's the vibe I'm trying to bring to my life. I've had enough drama and stress in the last year. My shitty ex screwed me out of our lease and forced me to go apartment searching when I had barely anything in the bank. Thankfully, my hometown was desperate for new teachers, so I got a hearty bonus and moving expenses included. It also helps that all my best friends are home. I will even be able to see one of my best friends get married toward the end of the summer.

I haven't seen the girls as much as I'd like to over the past few years. Not for lack of trying, but we've all been busy with school and work, and we're spread out all over. I'm glad we're all coming together to celebrate Alana and her fiancé. I missed a few of the wedding events this summer due to having to move out on a whim and find a new place, but now that all of that's done with, I'm looking forward to a bit of calm. I'm actually going to meet the girls for dinner tonight, and I can't wait.

I finish hanging the last banner and shut off the music. I grab all my stuff and lock up behind me.

After getting back to my apartment, I sigh when I see the mess and look around at the small space. I'm lucky to have found anything at all because a lot of the apartments in Lovers have filled up fast. My friend Heather wants to move back too, but she's stuck at Alana's guest house until she finds a place.

I swerve around the stacks of boxes until I find the one I'm looking for. I'm unusually super organized, and all my nice outfits are in a box labeled as such. I grab a dress and head to my bedroom. I've only been back for two weeks, but most of my place is already unpacked. I've just been trying to juggle getting ready for the school year with tidying up my space.

Once I'm showered, my hair is blow dried, and my skin is moisturized, I get dressed and ready to go. It's a casual night of dinner and drinks at Teddy's—the bar in town. Alana is too busy with her fiancé, Will, but Heather, Ryleigh, Norah, and I are still going. Norah offered to pick me up. It isn't unusual for her not to drink. I don't know how much she's even gone out since her husband, Finn, died last year.

I'm waiting outside when she pulls up.

"Kim! It's so good to see you." Norah pulls me in for a tight hug over the middle console.

"You look so great." I smile.

Norah has always had a way of looking pretty no matter what she was going through. She's just effortlessly beautiful. Her red hair is longer than I remembered it, and she's wearing a light blue sundress that complements her eyes.

"How has it been being back?" she asks.

"Weird. My parents moved away after I went to college, so I keep passing their house. One night I even turned into the driveway just out of routine." I laugh.

"It's even weirder when you see people you went to high school with, but they have kids and husbands and wives now. I swear, every time I go to the grocery store, I see five people we used to know," she jokes.

"Okay, well, I'll be avoiding the grocery store from now on."

"It's not so bad once you get used to it," she says.

She moved back shortly after Finn died. I think it was too much for her to be in the same house they had together.

"I'm so excited to see everyone tonight."

"It's all we've been talking about! We can't wait to have the gang fully back together."

"I wish Alana was coming tonight. I still haven't met her fiancé."

"He's okay. He's big into working and very traditional."

Norah says the words with a smile, but I can tell there's something off. I'm not sure if she'd tell me the truth if I asked, so I don't.

Norah and I make it to Teddy's and hurry in, excited to see the other girls.

"Kim!" Heather pulls me in for a hug the second she sees me. Ryleigh does the same, and we all grab a booth. I notice a familiar face behind the bar; is it possible that Alana's little sister is old enough to be a bartender?! Damn, that makes me feel old. I guess she's only a few years younger than us. I just always remember her tagging around and us being annoyed about it.

We order a round of drinks and way too many appetizers. Even though we were eating, I ate before we went out. Having celiac disease makes going out difficult. I'm used to it by now, but I don't want to risk contamination by eating something fried.

We all chat, and Heather and Norah tell us about what the townspeople have been up to. A lot of the conversation is gossip about the people we went to high school with, but I wouldn't have it any other way.

"So, you're teaching at the elementary school this year, right?" Heather turns the conversation to me.

"Yep. I have the hottest classroom in the building, but Miss Reese retired in the spring, so I got her room," I explain.

"Oh, my goodness, she was ready to retire when we were kids!" Norah laughs. It's true. No one knows exactly how old she is, but I heard she was more than happy to retire.

"I'm just glad I can decorate the way I want to this year." I smile.

"Let me guess, Harry Styles quotes?" Ryleigh asks before sipping her drink.

"Well, yeah," I mumble.

"I love how predictable you are, K. You never change, and I think that's something to celebrate." Ryleigh has a way of saying that like she means it as a compliment, but it sounds negative, too.

I excuse myself to the bathroom. Ryleigh and I are usually in sync, the closest of the group, but right now, her words hurt more than she knows. I know she meant well, but saying I'm predictable was kind of shitty. Maybe those words are just hitting harder since they're almost identical to the ones Billy said to me when we broke up. He wanted someone fun and exciting and who wanted to go on risky adventures. We'd been together two years, but I was boring for having a routine. I know what I like and that's what I stick to. Why does it matter that I don't try new things all that often?

"Hey, are you okay?" Heather walks in the bathroom and I sigh.

"I'm fine."

"You know Ryleigh didn't mean it the way she said it." She rubs my shoulder.

"I know." I nod.

I want to explain it to her, but she's standing next to me, and I know she wouldn't understand. She spent the last however long traveling and taking photos for a living. She takes tons of risks. I can't help it; taking risks makes me anxious.

Even cutting my hair makes me nervous.

Heather and I walk back to the table, and I pretend Ryleigh's words didn't hurt me. I'll call her tomorrow and talk it out. It isn't like we'll stop being friends over it, but I'm not one to sweep things under the rug. I didn't give her all the details when Billy and I broke up, so it makes sense that she wouldn't know that statement would hit a nerve. It's a joke a lot of my friends have made before.

It just cuts deeper now.

I'm the predictable one of the group. I have a good job, steady relationships, and I've worn the same shade of eye shadow since junior year of high school.

I enjoy my comfort zone. Sure, it can be sort of *lonely*, sometimes. It isn't like I want to be predictable, but I have a lot of anxiety, and trying to change what I like seems like a lot. I mean,

I get anxious at the thought of straying from my normal cocktail. I like it, why should I try something I might not like?

I always knew Billy wasn't the one. It was just comfortable, and I think that's why I let it go on for as long as I did. I wasn't surprised when he broke up with me. I was more upset that things were *changing*. I had to change almost everything I knew and loved about my life because we fell out of love. I had sort of hoped we could've carried on the way we were. Maybe not forever, but...no this is too sad. Would I have just stayed in a loveless relationship because I hate change?

Yeah. I probably would have.

I know I need to make some changes, but now I'm thinking I need something bigger. I start to make a list in my head of all the things I've wondered or thought about doing but never did. Maybe this summer I'll have the chance to cross a few things off so I'm no longer *predictable Kim*. I can take it slow, start with something easy, like trying a new cocktail, and work my way down the list.

I rejoin the group, not that it was too obvious I wasn't talking. I've always been the quiet one anyway. I make a mental note to change that, too. I have things to say, and I know my friends want to hear them. I just need to learn to use my voice. For some reason, I can dance like an idiot in front of twenty five-year-olds but not in front of my best friends.

That needs to change. Maybe Ryleigh's words were just what I needed to hear today.

THREE

Zara

"Hello, bestie! Have you met the love of your life yet?" Haley sing-songs from the other end of the phone. I can hear the hum of the New York City streets in the background, and I feel a little homesick.

"Would you stop that? I'm here to get shit done."

"So? You can have fun and get shit done."

"I'm *only* here to get shit done," I insist. It's pointless. Haley is a brick wall sometimes.

"Yeah, yeah. I'm thinking you'll meet her soon. I just feel it," she says confidently.

"Well, anyway. I was calling to see if you wanted a ticket to a LULY concert? It's next week. I forgot I even grabbed it, and obviously I'm not flying back for one night."

"You have a ticket to see the hottest lesbian singer right now, and you're willingly giving it to me? Am I being punk'd? Because that's not nice."

"I got a new ticket to see her show in September, but for now this ticket will go to waste if you don't take it."

"You don't have to ask me twice."

"You don't even know when it is."

"Who cares? I would call out sick to go." Truthfully, she's called out for less.

"Okay, I'm forwarding you the info."

"Have you seen more of the town? Is it still tiny and sad?"

"I never said it was sad. Just quaint. I don't think there's even a mall nearby. And there's, like, maybe two Uber drivers."

"That's insane!"

"I'm hoping I see some people our age or I'm going to be really bored this summer," I admit.

"Well, you have to go someplace people our age would be. Have you gone to the bar yet? A small town *has* to have a local bar."

"They do, and not yet. But I'll make that a priority." I laugh.

"Think about how we met most of our friends. We were usually drunk or high at some party or bar. We're social people, so you have to go be social to make friends. But don't make a new best friend, because I can't handle that."

"I know, you're my number one."

"Good, now I'm getting on the subway downtown so I'm going to lose you. Love you!"

I tell her I love her, but the phone call ends before I can finish. I think about what Haley said—maybe she was right. The most I've done is take Sandy on a walk and visit the local coffee shop. I've ordered takeout instead of eating in restaurants, and I haven't interacted with most of the people I've come across. I'm not going to learn about the town or find anyone my own age if I don't put myself out there. I just have to pretend this town is like…a tiny New York.

Or something.

I've been in Lovers a few days, and I have zero routine ironed out. I roll out of bed at different times every day and let life unfold before me. I suppose I do have one routine, Sandy's walk, which I'm about to do right now.

I grab her leash from the office, and Sandy comes running. It's a nice way to get my daily steps in and to see the town on foot. Sandy loves running in the sand; I've started to wonder if that's how she got her name. On most nights, we take a walk along the beach, and I even grab a ball to throw with her. She's running back and forth with the wet ball now, and I'm careful not to let her go swimming. I don't want Miss Taylor to have to worry about giving Sandy a bath when I bring her back.

As Sandy and I play, I start thinking about my next storyline. Maybe I can incorporate the beach into it. I try to focus, but nothing is coming to me. The lighthouse seems like a great place to put in a story, but I don't know enough about it yet. I have a tour scheduled for later in the week, so maybe I'll find some interesting facts that could potentially spark an idea for my book. There has to be at least one cool place my characters could hook up in the lighthouse.

Now that I think of it, it'll be hard for a dark romance to take place in a small town if everyone seems to know everyone. Unless…maybe the stalker is someone my main character knows but no one thinks twice about it. I guess I could use the childhood lovers trope or something similar. Now I wish I brought my laptop or journal with me to take notes. Hopefully I'll remember my ideas by the time I get back to the Inn.

I toss the ball across the beach, and Sandy runs for it. On her way back, she's so in the zone to bring it back to me that she doesn't see a woman walking in her path. I try to call out to the woman and warn her, but the second I do, Sandy collides with her. I race to them, hoping Sandy didn't do a number on her. How would I explain that to Miss Taylor?

"I'm so sorry! Are you okay?" I help the stranger up and my eyes lock with hers. *Fuck.* This woman is gorgeous.

"Yeah, I'm just a little sandy, that's all." Sandy hears her name and starts licking the woman's face, knocking her backward again.

"Sandy! Sit!" I reach for the woman again. "I'm sorry. Her name is Sandy. She thought you were talking to her."

"That's my bad, then." She laughs. Well, at least she isn't going to sue me.

"It's not even my dog. I'm just dog walking for the woman who owns the Inn. I'm from out of town." I smile. The woman in front of me has dark brown eyes and hair to match. She's wearing a pink romper and holding a pair of sandals.

"No worries. I'm Kim." She smiles, and I'm mesmerized for a second.

It's clearly been too long since I've been intimate with someone.

"Zara."

"Zara, that's a unique name."

"Hear a lot of unique names?"

"I do, actually. I'm a kindergarten teacher. Sometimes I have no idea what the child is saying, and not everyone spells things like they used to." She laughs.

"A kindergarten teacher, huh? I guess that means you're a local?"

"Oh, yes. Born and raised in Lovers. I just moved back, but I've basically lived here my whole life."

"I might have to pick your brain. I'm a writer in town to learn more about small towns." I don't usually throw out the author card so quickly, but sometimes it works. I don't know if it shows that I'm creative or that women love the idea of being someone's muse. Either way, it often leads to them screaming my name in bed.

"Wow, that's cool. I'm happy to answer any questions you might have."

"I have to keep walking Sandy, but would you like to walk with us? We can chat while I toss the ball for a bit?" I suggest. Kim looks at Sandy, and I take the moment to rake my eyes down her delicious body. She's thin, but she has breasts big enough to fit in the palms of my hands and legs that go on for days.

"Sure." She catches me looking, and I notice a blush across her cheeks.

"Come here, Sandy." I grab the ball from her and throw it again.

"So, just here for a bit then?" Kim asks.

"Yeah, I'm hoping to get inspired enough to plot my book and start the first draft."

"Is this your first book?"

"No, I have over a dozen out. But I'm switching subgenres, so it's a bit of a change. I'm from New York, and I know nothing about small towns," I confess.

"I've only been to New York once on a school trip, and it was... overwhelming to say the least."

"The city definitely isn't for everyone." I shrug.

"Same could be said about small towns," she points out.

We keep talking for a bit, until Sandy starts to slow down. I can tell she's ready to head back, but I'm not done with Kim. We talked about small towns for what felt like the last hour, but only minutes have passed. I've been able to pick her brain a bit, and she seems to like the questions I've asked. I'm sure that's just a side effect of being a teacher.

I've been debating the best way to ask if she wants to come back to the Inn with me. I have no idea if she likes women, but my gaydar has never failed me in the past. Maybe I can get her talking a little more before I ask.

I re-leash Sandy and pause to look at Kim.

"Can I walk back with you? I parked up there." She points by the parking lot that's near the steps up to the Inn.

"Of course." It gives me another minute to come up with a reason to get her to come back with me. I'm really not usually so bad at this, but for some reason, Kim makes me nervous. Maybe it's because I'm out of practice. I don't want to think about how long it's been since I've been with anyone. If it weren't for my vibrator, my pussy would be filled with cobwebs.

"Do you walk on the beach every night?" I ask.

"I used to. I've been trying to get out of my routine." She frowns.

"Why's that?"

"One of my friends made a point that I haven't changed much in the last several years. And that I'm a bit boring." She sighs.

"I don't believe that one bit." I huff.

"Really?" Her eyes light up.

"Maybe you haven't changed a ton, but who says that's a bad thing? And why would they say you're boring?" I ask.

"Well, they just said predictable. But they aren't exactly wrong…" It almost seems like she wants to elaborate, but she doesn't.

"So, just start being unpredictable."

"What do you mean?"

"I once spent a month saying *yes* to every experience I was offered. I've never regretted that. Maybe just start doing things out of your comfort zone."

"Hm." Kim stops walking, and I think it's because we're almost at the parking lot.

Then she grabs me by the waist and pulls me in for a kiss. Her lips melt into mine, and it takes me a second to register what's happening before I kiss her back. I grab her by the hips and pull her into me. Letting go of the leash, I silently pray Sandy wouldn't use this moment to run away from me. If we're doing this, we're doing it right. She slides her tongue in my mouth and groans when I suck on her tongue. Kim slowly pulls away with hooded eyes, and I smile. God, this was the last thing I had anticipated when I left my room today.

Fuck. Does this mean Haley was right? No. I don't believe in muses or meeting random strangers being anything more than what it is. Haley is the romantic, I'm just the romance author. I can be romantic when I need to be, and I'm not a cynic by any means, but I'm a realist. I know Kim and I aren't going to magically fall in love, and I doubt she will end up being the answer to all my writing problems, but maybe the two of us can have a few hours of fun. I'd love to get out of my own head by giving someone else head…

"Will you come back to my room with me?" I finally throw it out there, being as blunt as possible.

"Yes." Kim doesn't think about it. She just nods, and I hold out my hand. I have a feeling I'll be hearing that word a lot more in the next few hours.

FOUR

Kim

I don't know what came over me. But I'm tired of being too afraid to do things. I'm tired of being called predictable. I'm almost thirty, and I've never even had a one-night stand. Isn't that like, a bucket list thing? Maybe that's what I should do. Make a list of things I've always thought about doing but was too afraid to actually do. That would show everyone who dared to call me predictable. It felt so good to kiss Zara; what was I afraid of anyway? Maybe all the things I want to do will turn out the way this did. I mean, not everything I want to do is sex-related, but this seems like a good place to start.

I've only been in serious monogamous relationships throughout my entire adult life. There's nothing wrong with that, but what if I want more? I don't want to suddenly get old and always wonder what-if. My friends are all unpredictable, and I want to be more like them. So, I followed Zara toward the Inn, and she dropped off Sandy with her owner before leading me upstairs.

"I should warn you, there's no elevator. And unfortunately, I'm not strong enough to carry you up three flights." Zara winks, and I blush. I haven't been with a woman in a bit, but it has to be like riding a bike, right?

"No problem," I say, even though by the time we reach her floor, I'm trying to steady my breath. Those stairs were no joke.

Zara slides her key and then holds the door open for me. The room is in a bit of disarray. There are clothes on the bed, the couch, and the floor. The TV was left on, and the bed definitely wasn't made today. At least I know Zara wasn't trolling the beach waiting to find someone to take back with her.

"I clearly wasn't expecting company." She quickly starts tidying the bed, tossing it all in the closet.

"No worries, I'm not here for that."

"Oh? And what might you be here for then?" Zara returns to my side with a devilish look.

"I should admit, I've never done this before," I say quickly. I'm not as suave as I'm pretending to be, and suddenly, all my nerves are hitting me at once.

"Been with a woman?" Zara takes a step back and raises an eyebrow.

"No, I dated a woman for three years. I just meant I've never had a one-night stand before."

"Ah, well, I'm happy to walk you through it, if you'd like." She smirks.

I nod. My mouth is suddenly too dry to speak. Zara pushes my bangs to the side and brushes her hand across my cheek. Sparks ignite as I feel her touch on my skin.

"I'm going to need you to use your words, Sweetie." She tilts her head, her blonde hair flowing behind her. She has piercing blue eyes, and even though she isn't wearing any makeup, her eyelashes look to be miles long.

"Yes, please," I say quietly.

Zara leans in, and I feel her cool breath along my lips. I close my eyes. Her soft lips press against mine, and I melt into her. My hands reach for her waist, and I pull her close to me. She slips her tongue in my mouth, and I groan. Her hands are on the sides of my face, holding me close to her, but it doesn't seem like enough. I forgot how much I loved kissing women until now. It's nothing compared to kissing a man. Like, that's fun, but kissing a woman is magical.

Zara leads me to the bed, and I sit on the edge. She keeps kissing me while her hands begin to roam. One hand grazes the top of my breasts while the other sits steadily on my thigh. I reach for her hips and drag my hands up her body until I'm at her chest. I take her boobs in my hands and moan into her mouth. God, I'm so needy right now. Heat is pooling between my legs. It's been too long since I've had sex—*good* sex. Toward the end, with Billy, we didn't even bother with each other. He'd go in the shower and get off, and I'd use my vibrator in the bed. It was easier, and honestly, more fun. But *this*? This feels like heaven. Zara only just started touching me, and I'm already on edge.

"God, you're so hot," Zara murmurs as she nibbles at my earlobe. I get a whiff of her strawberry shampoo and groan as she begins kissing down my neck.

"Can you give me a hint as to where the zipper or buttons are so I can get you out of this thing?" Zara asks, pulling back. I whimper at the loss of contact, but I laugh.

"The zipper's in the back." I stand up to turn around and she pushes me back on the bed.

"That's better." Zara straddles my hips and leans in to whisper in my ear. She slowly drags down the zipper all the way to my ass. She places kisses all down my back and grazes the top of my panties.

"I think you need to take this off now," Zara commands. I'm not normally one to be so submissive, but fuck, the way she said it makes me want to give her everything.

I stand and let the romper fall to my feet. I'm not wearing a bra, so I instinctively cover my chest with my arms and Zara reaches for me.

"Don't cover up; you're beautiful." She slowly moves my arms and sits on the bed, looking at me. Her eyes rake over every inch of me, as if trying to commit my body to memory. Is this what it feels like to be truly desired?

Instead of waiting for her to make another move, I decide to take charge a bit. Zara's wearing jean shorts and a crop top. I drop to my knees and start unbuttoning her shorts. She lifts her ass to let them free, and I toss them to the side. She's wearing a pair of cotton panties that are covered in flowers. They'd be cute —except for the wet spot right in the middle. She wants this just as much as I do. I relax a bit as I lean in and start kissing her thighs.

"Is this okay?" I look up at her, ready to stop if she says the word.

"Oh, yes." She nods.

I brush my lips across her wet panties, and her hips buck instantly closer to me. Zara gasps and I smile as I push her hips back on the bed. Hooking my arms under her thighs, I lean in to tease her. I place kisses on her inner thighs, grazing my teeth across the waistband of her panties and inhaling her sweet scent. When she's wiggling too much, I decide to put her out of her misery and taste her. I push her panties to the side and dive in, tongue first.

"Oh!" Zara yelps as my tongue connects with her clit.

I slide my tongue up and down her dripping folds. Her body reacts to my every touch. Zara's hand grips my hair tightly, and I moan against her. She tastes even better than I imagined. Sliding my tongue inside her, I bury my face in her pussy. She pushes my face closer to her center, and I feel her tightening against my tongue. I move one hand from under her thighs so I can touch her clit, run my fingers through her folds to wet them, and then rub small circles on her clit. Zara instantly reacts.

"Holy shit!" She whimpers, and as I continue, I feel her clenching around my tongue.

Zara curses as she comes on my face, her thighs shaking and her body jolting. I don't let up until she lets go of my hair and pushes me away. She's lying on the bed like she just ran a marathon, so I quickly wipe off my face with a tissue and stretch my legs. My knees aren't as good as they used to be. Someone should warn you—once you hit twenty-five, there's a big decline in how low you can go.

"Wow," Zara whispers. I lie next to her, and she smiles.

"Give me a second to recover, and I will happily return the favor." Zara gets up and walks over to the desk, returning with two water bottles.

"Here." She hands me one, and I take a hearty sip.

She holds out her hand for the bottle and places them both on the nightstand. I watch her ass shake as she moves, biting down on my bottom lip. I taste the remnants of her on me, and I groan. Zara turns around and smirks at me.

"See something you like?" she teases as she climbs back into the bed. Crawling over to my lap, she straddles me.

"Oh, yes. Something I like a lot," I admit. This is casual. I don't need to hide how attracted to her I am. I'll probably never see her again.

Zara pushes her dark hair behind her ears and smiles down at me. She brushes her hands up my bare chest, and I suck in a breath. Her fingers are like magic, and I'm eagerly awaiting the next trick. She leans in to kiss me, her lips taking control of mine. She falls back into me, both of us lost in the sheets as we explore each other. I touch her breasts, pulling softly on her nipples and feeling the way she reacts to me. She slides her body between my thighs, and I swear I stop breathing.

Every nerve I have is heightened as she looks at me with desire. My pussy drips down my thighs as she looks at me. I suddenly feel self-conscious; I didn't shave or wax. But it's not like I planned this. I think this is the most spontaneous thing I've ever done in my entire life. Zara must see me tense, because she looks up from where she was kissing my thighs and tilts her head.

"What's up? Do you want me to stop?"

"No, no. I just... I'm sorry I didn't, like, shave or anything. I clearly didn't expect—" Zara cuts me off with a smile.

"Kim, if you think a little natural body hair is going to stop me from devouring you, you're mistaken. You can be your authentic self with me."

"Okay."

"So you want me to continue?" Zara checks and I nod.

"Yes," I say, realizing she's waiting for a verbal confirmation.

Zara dips between my thighs, and I moan when her warm mouth connects with my hot center. She sucks gently on my clit, and I gasp. My head falls back into the pillows, and Zara presses her tongue along my pussy. Her fingers slide around and slip into me. She uses her free hand to press right over my pubic bone, and I swear, I almost come that second. It's all too much at once, and she knows exactly what she's doing.

"Hold on babe," she says, looking up at me.

I know she says something else, but I can't hear her. I'm too busy memorizing this scene. Zara between my thighs, her face slick with my wetness, and her fingers pumping in and out of me. My body is slipping away from me, and the stars are coming just as she goads me to finish for her. In this moment, I'd do anything she asks of me.

"Yes! Yes! Yes!" I scream.

Zara kisses my clit as I come. My eyes are clamped shut through my climax. If all one-night stands could be like this, maybe this is something I need to do more often.

FIVE

Zara

I walk into town earlier than I expected. It's barely ten a.m., and I'm already out and about for the day. I have my fully charged laptop, my headphones, and two brand-new journals. One is for plotting, and the other is for random journaling and scrapbooking.

I order a large iced black coffee and find a table in the middle of the cafe. It's the perfect spot because I can position my chair to see the entire cafe. Today, I'm in people-watching mode. I need to get a vibe of the way small-town people live, and part of that will come from watching the patrons. I'm always amazed by the kind of things I see and hear when I actually take the time to listen. I often put on my headphones but don't play anything; instead, I listen to nearby conversations. I'm never going to write about the things I hear, but it gets me into the heads of different people.

So, as I sit down, I pull out a felt-tip pen and start a new page in my journal. I write the date, and then I get to people-watching. I write down everything I see, hear, and smell. I want to capture this cafe as best as I can so I can remember what it's like in a bustling cafe in a small town. Sure, bustling means ten people compared to my normal Starbucks back home that has at least ten new customers per minute. Still, I write down descriptions of clothes, voices, tones, accents—everything.

When I've run out of things to watch and can feel my attention slipping away, I close my notebook and start up my laptop. I take a bite of the protein bar from my bag and take a large sip of my coffee. I need brain food if I'm going to focus. I need to have an outline as soon as possible, and every time I start one, I have a tendency to delete it. I know I'm hard on myself, but I also know I can do better. If I don't push myself, who will?

I open my plotting app, pull out my mood board, and turn on my writing playlist. I start writing some ideas down, some of which I'm sure I'll delete later. But at least I'm writing things down. I have the darker elements of the romance planned in my head. My main character's ex-boyfriend is going to be a stalker, and her new girlfriend is going to save the day. There will be a ton of spicy scenes and some rope and knife play. My readers love those scenes the most, and I don't want to let them down. Plus, they're fun to write.

I start writing the description of my first female main character. I don't have a name for her yet, but I can see what she looks like in my head. Long, flowing brunette hair, high cheekbones, and dark brown eyes. She has a small figure, but she's tall—with amazingly long legs. As I start writing it down, I stop myself. Subconsciously, I'm writing about Kim. I just described her to a T, and now I have to start over.

Sure, I've thought about her once or twice since our time together. She's sexy as hell in a nerdy kind of way. We didn't exchange info, though, and I'm not here looking for a relationship or anything.

Then again, if she and I happen to see each other again, I wouldn't say no to a repeat of our first night together. Maybe that's something she wants too. My thighs clench as I think about how good she tasted and the way she responded to my touch. I hadn't been with anyone in a while, and she's addictive.

Suddenly, I get the urge to start writing. I'm not entirely sure where I'm going with it, but it's a good start. The main couple meet on the beach, and the spark grows from there. I know it sounds like how Kim and I met, but it isn't like Kim will read this. She doesn't even know what my pen name is—or the title of any of my books. As far as she knows, I'm an unknown author. It works in my favor most of the time. I mean, who'd want to have a one-night stand be able to find out everything about them from a website? But in a case like this, where I sort of wish Kim had a way to reach out, it sucks.

Oh, well. It's probably all for the best.

Three cups of iced coffee later, I decide to head back to the Inn. Except, I notice a bookstore on the way. I stop in and head for the dark romance section. I can't help it; I like to know if my books are there, and sometimes I sign them if I can.

I peruse the shop and find three of my latest book in stock, so I carry them up to the front and wait in line.

"Hi, I was wondering if I could—"

"Oh, my gosh! You're Zara Grey!" The petite redhead behind the counter squeals. Thankfully, no one else seems to know who I am, or if they do, they don't care.

"Yeah, I was wondering if I could sign these?" I hold up the books.

"Oh, heck yes!" She grabs a marker and walks around the counter to me. "I'm sorry. I'm such a huge fan. I'm always devouring your books! I'm Norah."

"I appreciate that, it's always nice to meet a fan." I smile. She hands me the marker, and I sign my name in each. Then I take a photo to share on social media. I won't share that I'm visiting all summer, but I can say I stopped in. I always like to help small businesses, especially bookstores.

"I know my boss would kill me if I didn't ask. Is there any chance you'll be around longer than today?"

I must look at her weird, because she quickly backs up and explains herself.

"We'd just love to have you do a signing in the store. We love when authors happen to pass through and want to sign something."

"Oh, yeah. I'll be here the rest of the summer. You can email me, and we can arrange something." I try to stay vague. Not that I think Norah is some crazy fan, but I've heard horror stories about stalkers, and I don't need to go down that road. I like writing about them, not having one.

"This is amazing, thank you so much." She tucks the paper into her front pocket and smiles.

"Would you like a photo together?" I ask, because I have a feeling she's not allowed to.

"Would you?!" Her eyes widen in excitement.

"Of course." She takes out her phone and puts it on selfie mode. She snaps a photo and thanks me.

"No worries! Do you want me to put these back on the shelf?"

"No, I'm going to add them to the front table. We have a spot for signed copies. They usually sell even faster," Norah explains.

"Perfect. I'm going to look around for a bit." I hand her the marker and head to the other side of the store.

I walk along the back wall, looking at all the different sections of books. It's surprisingly large for how small the space looked outside. But with high ceilings, they make it work. I browse the new releases before I come across the stationary section. I don't *need* a new journal, but it isn't like it'll hurt just to look. I love the feel of a new journal in my hands. The possibility, the beauty. Even if it might sit on a shelf for months before I actually use it. I stop myself from actually buying any of them, no matter how pretty they are.

Since I'm not buying a journal or a book, I decide to get a

magnet for my collection. My fridge back home is covered in magnets from various places I've visited. I want to support this shop in some way, even though I know this won't be the last time I'll be here.

"We usually have more of a selection, but tourist season clears us out," Norah says, looking at the magnet.

"I like this one, it's cute." It's just a bookshelf with the store name, *To Be Loved Bookshop* in pretty letters.

Norah hands me a small paper bag, and I slip it in my bag. I walk back to the Inn. It's a bit of a walk, but I'm used to New York City blocks that are sometimes miles long. I like getting my steps in.

"Hello, Zara. Did you have a nice day?" Miss Taylor is in the lobby of the Inn, wiping down the front coffee table.

"I did! I worked at the cafe in town and then stopped at the bookshop." I smile.

"Oh, isn't it lovely? I try to visit when I can. I've never been a reader, but I do like to look at the pretty covers."

I laugh. If only she knew what I do for a living.

"I'm going to head up to relax a bit, but I'll be down later for Sandy and her walk."

"Sounds good, let me know if you need fresh sheets or anything."

"Okay." I nod.

I head upstairs, slip into my room, and toss my stuff on the desk. I open the curtains all the way and let the sun shine in. Then, I strip out of my clothes and climb into the bed naked. Nothing beats climbing into a cool bed after being out all day. I pick up my phone and scroll social media for a while. I have an amazing assistant who is on top of my author profiles, so I rarely logged into those. Readers aren't always kind in the comments, often forgetting there are real people on the other sides of the screen. I typically use a burner account to enjoy content on my own.

I'll have to make some content for her at some point this

summer. But for now, she's reusing what I gave her before I left New York.

My phone is starting to die, so I plug it in and look for the TV remote. I turn it on to an old episode of *Friends*, and I tune it out mostly.

Kim is the only thing on my mind right now. My pillows still smell like her. It's flowery and sweet with notes of roses and vanilla. If I ever see her again, I'll have to ask what kind of perfume she uses. I've been falling asleep every night, smelling it as if she's still here. I hadn't expected her to be gone that morning, but she had said what it was from the start—a one-night stand. I knew we weren't going to turn into anything, but I wouldn't have minded one more chance to make her scream for me. Kim is beautiful and sexy and seems perfect for me. Maybe, with any luck, we'll somehow see each other again. I wouldn't mind the opportunity to tie her to the bed or try out some of my toys with her. I didn't bring my full collection, but I did bring along two of my favorites.

I'm getting wet just thinking about her. I rub my thighs together and groan. Maybe it wouldn't hurt to get some of this sexual tension out of me. I reach for the toy sitting on the nightstand and turn it on. Closing my eyes, I imagine the sexy brunette slipping between my thighs.

SIX

Kim

I left Zara the other morning, and I haven't been able to stop thinking about her—about all the things she did to me and how my body felt. I can close my eyes and still feel how good she made me feel. I'm getting sex flashbacks like crazy. My panties are consistently a mess, and I have to keep distracting myself. Well, during the day at least. I use my vibrator every night, replaying every second from memory over in my head. Part of me wishes I had the courage to go over to the Inn and see her again. But I don't want to be the clingy girl who can't understand the meaning of a one-night stand. Besides, it isn't like I have any way of contacting her—aside from just showing up like a weirdo. I snuck out of her room that next morning, and that was that.

"Kim, does the dress fit okay?" Alana calls out, and I remember where I am. The little shop just outside of Lovers, trying on my bridesmaid's dress for her wedding.

"Yup! I think so, I just need some help with the zipper." I open the door, and Alana smiles, looking me over. I spin around so she can finish the zipper, and then I walk out.

It's just the two of us today because everyone else has already had their dresses sized. But I don't mind, plus, I'm going to get to see Alana's dress today, too.

"Do you like it?" Alana looks at my face to make sure I'm telling the truth.

"I really do. I wasn't sure about the front, but it's perfect," I admit. I'm not usually a fan of low-cut tops, but somehow this is classy and not slutty.

"Okay, good. I just want everyone to be comfortable." She smiles. It's her day, but she's still worried about how everyone else feels.

"I think the color complements your skin tone. I tried to pick a color that would be good for everyone."

"Did everyone else like theirs?"

"Yes. I think Ryleigh needs hers resized, but Heather and Gemma's are good to go." She smiles. Gemma is Alana's college best friend. We met in passing at Alana's college graduation party.

"Okay, I'll go change, and then you can show me your dress. I'm excited to see it!" I gush.

"Sure." Alana nods. I can tell there's something off with her, but I'm not entirely sure what it is.

I head back into the dressing room and change back into my normal clothes—a T-shirt with a cute pun about animals and a pair of tan shorts. I give my dress to the worker, and she brings it to the front to ring it up before we leave. I have more time before I need to come pick it up and have my final fitting. I have a feeling I won't forget since Alana has been sending us weekly reminders.

I grab a seat in front of the mirrors and wait for Alana to come out. It takes her a few minutes, but I'm sure it's because it's a more intricate dress than mine. I scroll through my phone, and I wonder, once again, about Zara. She said she's an author, but I doubt she goes by her real name. I search "author Zara" on Instagram anyway, just in case. Nothing pops up, and I sigh, locking my phone. Maybe I'm not meant to see her again. I mean, it isn't like I'd follow her on Instagram and message her even if I did find her. I know my place, and I refuse to let mind-blowing sex get in the way of my successful one-night stand.

Alana finally walks out, and I'm in awe of her dress. It's long-sleeved but dips down to show off her ample cleavage. The dress is white with an upper layer of lace flowers covering her arms and chest. It flows all around her; she looks like a princess. It looks perfect on her, but her smile isn't genuine. It looks more forced than excited. Maybe it isn't what she thought it would look like? Or maybe it doesn't feel comfortable?

"Are you okay?" I stand up and walk over to Alana.

"Yeah." She nods but it's not very convincing.

"What's wrong? Is it the dress? Because you look beautiful."

"No, I just have so much going on right now. The wedding has put a lot on my plate. It's just stressful." She sighs. Alana plays with the lace between her fingers as I search for the right thing to say.

"Is Will helping with all the planning? I know you wanted to do a lot by yourself but…"

"He's got a lot going on, too. He needs to make sure his company is running smoothly so we can go on our honeymoon without interruptions."

"But still, you're working, and you can't do it all by yourself. I'm around to help as much as I can."

"It'll be fine. I'm just stressed, that's all."

"A, it's okay if you're stressed. But if it's something more, you can talk to me about it." I reach for her, and she sighs.

"I'm fine." She pulls back and disappears into the dressing room.

I sit back down and sigh. I'm not one to push. It just isn't my style. I have too much of my own anxiety to try and fix someone else's. I just feel bad that Alana is struggling. The girls and I help as much as we can, without stepping on her toes, of course. Maybe there's more we can do without her knowing? Like take over some of the tasks she's stressing about. I'm just not sure how we can find out what those tasks are. Gemma is her maid of honor, and I know she hasn't been asked to do much. Alana is a bit of a control freak, and we love that about her, but it doesn't allow for much room to help her.

"Are you ready?" Alana asks.

"Yeah." I jump up.

Following her to the front, I listen as she discusses the particulars with the staff, and we head out. She gave me a ride here, so I slide into the passenger seat and buckle up.

"Wanna go get a coffee? I have a major caffeine headache," Alana says as she gets in.

"Coffee sounds great." I smile.

"I'm glad you like your dress. I wanted to pick something that everyone would like. I mean, I know I gave you choices, but I'm glad it was so easy for everyone."

"You somehow managed to pick the most flattering bridesmaids dresses to ever exist," I admit.

"It wasn't simple, that's for sure. They kept pushing me toward stuff with ruffles and puffy sleeves. I was like, we're not a hundred years old, we're barely thirty. We need hot dresses." Alana laughs.

"You said that to the owner?" I think of the little old lady I saw today sewing the dresses in the back.

"Yes. She laughed with me and picked these out."

"That's amazing. I guess she knew exactly what to do once you told her what was up."

We get to the coffee shop and notice it's super busy. "Crap, there's no parking. Do you wanna go in and grab the coffees, and we can head back to your place?"

"Sure." I nod. My stomach tightens thinking about Alana in the mess of my apartment, but it isn't like she doesn't know I *just* moved back.

Alana tries to hand me her wallet, but I wave her off. I can afford to pay for a five-dollar cup of coffee.

I head inside Love in a Cup and look at the menu. Alana

said she'd text me her order, but I'm not sure what I want. Well, that isn't quite true. I know what I want: a vanilla cold brew iced coffee. I'm just trying to push myself out of my comfort zone and be less predictable. It worked well with Zara, so maybe I'll find a new coffee order, too. The salted caramel iced latte sounds good, so I brace myself for change and order a medium along with Alana's iced cold brew with almond milk.

As I wait for our coffee, I look around the shop. It's a cute place with lots of seats and tables, even spots to plug in electronics. The girls and I used to come here in high school and study together. But as I'm glancing around the array of dates, moms with kids, and teenagers, I spot a familiar blonde. She's staring intently at her computer with her headphones on, and I freeze. Should I go over and say hi? *No!* That isn't something a one-night stand would do, right? I mean, I should just be playing it cool. God, I wish Alana had come in instead of me. I'm never coming here again.

I know I shouldn't be freaking out, but I don't want to do the *wrong* thing. I'd never had a one-night stand before, and I sure as hell never encountered the person in public a few days later. I don't know why this didn't occur to me. Zara said she'd be in town for the rest of the summer, and it isn't like Lovers is a big town. I guess I forgot that the odds of running into someone you know are extraordinarily higher when you don't want to see them.

"Kim!" the barista calls my name for my order, and I smile.

I grab the two coffees and head to the station with the straws and napkins. They only have paper straws, which are fine, but I have to look at the label to make sure they're gluten-free. Gluten gets snuck into so many things for no reason. While I'm glad the turtles are safe from these straws, I might not be.

"Kim?" a soft voice says as a hand touches my bare shoulder.

"Zara, hi." I smile awkwardly. Is she going to think I stalked her and found her here? Oh, God.

"I'm happy to see you again. Are you just getting coffee to go?" Zara notices the cups.

"Oh, yeah, my friend Alana is waiting in the car. There wasn't any parking, so I just ran in," I explain. It feels like I'm saying too many words, but I also can't stop myself. Zara makes me incredibly nervous.

"Makes sense, I thought you might just have a caffeine addiction. Not that I'm one to talk." She laughs. Her lips are colored a beautiful bright red, and she's wearing a pair of oversized glasses that make her look super cute.

"Are you here working?" I ask, glancing at her computer.

"Sort of. I've been plotting more than actually writing, though."

"That's still considered working." I smile. I'm not sure what to say in this situation. She seems happy to see me, but that doesn't necessarily mean she *wants* to see me again.

"So, I know you had mentioned this being a one-night stand. But would you be up for doing something again this summer? I had fun with you." Zara brushes her hand along my forearm, and I melt.

"Uh yeah, that'd be cool." I nod, trying to sound casual but probably sounding anything but.

"Okay, cool. I'll give you my number, and we can plan something. Sound good?"

"Yeah." I slip my phone out of my pocket, unlock it, and hand it to her. She adds her number in and sends herself a text.

"My phones on the table, but I'll be sure to text you back later." She winks and I swear my panties are garbage at this point. How can someone just ooze sex appeal like this?

Zara walks back to the table, and I'm no better than a man when I stare as she walks away. Her ass sways in her tight black shorts. The thought of getting to touch her again…

God, I'm in trouble.

SEVEN

Zara

I get the text that Kim's here and head downstairs to meet her. We've been texting a lot the last few days—ever since I ran into her at the cafe. She was so nervous when we ran into each other; it was kind of cute. I didn't know if she'd be too nervous to see me again, but thankfully, she was on the same page as me. Neither of us want anything serious right now, but we can both go for something fun and easy. I try not to miss any steps as I race down the stairs to meet her. She's sitting in the lobby, holding her phone, and she looks up the second I reach her.

"Hey." She smiles, her dark eyes lighting up when she sees me.

"Hi." I reach for her and press my lips to her cheek. She blushes at my touch, and I laugh lightly. God, she's so sexy.

Even now, in a summery, light green wrap dress, she's still effortlessly beautiful. She somehow makes it look sexy as hell. I want to rip it off her and eat her out on the couch.

"Why don't we go up?" I suggest, and she nods. She's quieter than last time, but I assume she's nervous again.

We reach my room, and I kick off my shoes by the door. I've cleaned up a bit this time, since I knew she was coming over. I put the lights on but dim them a bit and close the curtains. I don't want to give anyone on the beach a free show. I turn around to offer Kim a drink, and she smiles at me. She pulls at the string on her wrap dress, and it slowly comes undone. The green fabric hits the floor, but my eyes are locked on her body.

Kim's wearing bright red lingerie that leaves nothing to the imagination. Her breasts are falling out of the lace cups, her light skin peeking through the material. It looks like a tiny skirt with red ruffles on the bottom, and I'm in awe. I think my mouth is hanging open, and I don't even care. This woman is unbelievable. I have no words to describe the desire I'm feeling. This woman has effectively taken away an author's words.

"Wow," I finally manage, stepping toward her.

"You like?" She smiles.

"Oh, I fucking *love*." I groan, touching the tops of her thighs and playing with the red ruffles.

"I thought it would be fun, but no one warns you when you dress like this, it's cold as hell on your ass when you drive." Kim laughs.

I spin her around and take in the back of the outfit. Fuck. It's tied like an apron around her waist, and there's nothing but a thin red string between her full cheeks. I grab her ass with one hand and squeeze tightly.

"I wanted to fuck you the second I saw you, but damn." I don't let go of her ass but spin her back around so I can kiss her.

"I felt like being bold." She blushes.

I grab her cheeks with one hand and turn her face to look at me. "You should always follow that instinct."

Before she can answer, I lean in and press my lips to hers. She pushes against me, grinding our hips together. The lace feels delicate under my fingers. I resist the urge to rip it to shreds, knowing firsthand how expensive nice lingerie can be. I slide my hands around both ass cheeks and grab handfuls of her voluptuous ass. Kim groans as I pick her up, and she wraps both her legs around my waist. I'm not a bodybuilder by any means, but I go to the gym enough to stay in shape. Picking up a woman and carrying her to the bed while she kisses you has to be one of the hottest things in life. I toss Kim onto the bed when we get to it, and she falls back with a smile.

"God, I can't get over how gorgeous you are," I say aloud.

Kim blushes and I bury my face in her neck. Placing kisses up and down the nape of her neck. She groans with each one, her fingers finding the hem of my shirt and pulling the fabric over my head. I'm not wearing a bra, so the cool air instantly hits my hardened nipples. Kim reaches for my breasts, but I pull back. I want to focus on her first this time, and I can't do that if she's touching me.

"This is all about you first, baby." I prop her arms over her head. They're not tied, so she can technically move, but she doesn't. Instead, she waits for me to make another move.

I kiss her lips again, tasting her sweet strawberry ChapStick. I reach for the tops of her breasts peeking out from her lingerie and slide the cups down just enough to see her nipples. I take one in my mouth, pulling it between my teeth, and Kim moans under me. I take turns going back and forth between her breasts until I feel her squirming under me. She's moving her hips, hoping to get more friction from me.

"Can I taste you?" I ask, looking up at her from between her breasts. She nods, but I wait patiently until she speaks the word out loud.

I slowly slide down her stomach and press my face into her pretty pussy. Kim's hips instantly buck, and I can smell her arousal. Fuck, it's almost as good as I remember. I brush my lips across her thong. The tiny piece of fabric does nothing to hide her lips and wetness. It's basically a soaked piece of cloth at this point. But instead of taking it off, I slide my tongue across it and watch as Kim moans under me. I slip my tongue behind the fabric, licking the lips of her pussy, and groan. God, how the hell does this woman taste so good?

"Oh, fuck!" Kim squeals.

"Mmm," I hum against her.

I use my hands to pull the fabric to the side and attach my lips to her clit. I suck softly, just enough to tease her, and she whimpers. Her hands reach for my head and brush through my hair. Slipping my tongue down her center, I taste all of her. Flattening my tongue, I move it up and down her pussy, feeling her desire deepen. Kim grabs tightly on my hair as my nose brushes against her clit. I move my fingers to tease her, playing in her wetness. Once they're nice and wet, I look up at Kim and hold them out for her.

"Lick them clean," I command.

"You want me to t-taste myself?" She shivers as she asks.

"I want you to know how good you taste."

She hesitates but then leans forward, taking both my fingers in her mouth. She sucks and licks them clean. If I had a dick, I'd be asking for head right about now, because *wow*. She bites down on her bottom lip, and I can tell by her bright blush that she likes the way she tastes.

I use two fingers to dip inside her. Motioning forward, I hook my fingers inside, hitting her G-spot, and she goes wild for me. I latch my mouth onto her clit, and she screams my name. Her hands tighten around my hair again, holding my head down as I suck on her. Her legs begin to shake, and I can only hear the sounds of her moans.

"Oh, yes! Fuck, Zara! Right there! Oh, yes!" she cries out the words, only spurring me on.

I'm clenching my thighs together, feeling the wetness seep from my panties and down my thighs. I'm so fucking turned on. Still, I'm determined to make her come for me. I want to taste every inch of her. I pump my fingers just a little bit harder, and she comes undone for me.

"YES!" she screams, and I don't let up. Even when she goes limp, I take one last lick before joining her on the pillows.

"Oh, fuck." She turns over to look at me.

"You're so incredible," I murmur.

She blushes and closes her eyes. I reach for the water I left on the nightstand and take a sip. I put it back and hand the other one to her. She looks drunk on orgasms, and we're only getting started.

"I guess the lingerie was a good choice," she jokes.

"Oh, yes. Please only wear that from now on. Do you have anything you love doing in bed?"

"Um, that. What we just did? Ten outta ten." Kim laughs.

"I'm serious. Any hidden kinks or things you've wanted to try but were afraid to?"

"Hmm." Kim pauses to think about it. "I've thought about being tied up before, but I never really trusted anyone else to do it."

"Would you trust me?"

"Do you have rope?"

"Is it weird if I say yes?" I grimace. "I'm a romance author, sometimes I need certain toys and things to try so I can describe them better."

"That makes sense. I was hoping it wasn't to tie me up and kill me." Kim laughs.

"Not at all. I write romance, not thrillers." We both laugh in unison, and it feels comfortable—nice.

"Do you think we could another time? I mean, if there is another time? Fuck, I'm really screwing up this one-night stand thing aren't I?" Kim turns as red as her lingerie.

"Look, I'm only here for the summer so I don't want to lead you on or anything, but if you'd like to be friends with benefits this summer and do stuff like this"—I motion between us—"I'd love to."

"Friends with benefits; I like the sound of that."

"Then you just let me know when you're ready to try ropes, but until then, no rush."

"Okay." Kim nods. "But I'd really like to fuck you now."

"Any position in particular?"

"I'd kill to have you sit on my face."

"You sure as hell don't have to ask me twice." I shimmy out of my shorts and panties and toss them aside.

Kim positions herself on the pillows and smiles at me. I climb on top of her and hover slightly over her. Before I can steady myself, Kim tugs me down by my thighs, gripping me tightly. Her lips brush against my pussy, and I have to catch myself with the headboard. Gripping it tightly, I begin to rock my hips slowly as Kim licks me. Her tongue does circles around my clit, dips inside me, and slides up and down before starting all over again. She's taking her time and building me up. It would be torturous if it didn't feel so good.

"Fuck, I love your tongue," I moan out.

She mumbles something under me, but all I can see are her closed eyes and my pussy grinding against her mouth. Kim slips her tongue inside me, and I almost collapse. She grips my ass, and I rock forward, needing more friction.

"Fuck! Right there! Please don't stop!" I cry out.

Kim keeps going, keeping the same pace as I ride out my orgasm. There's a tightening in my stomach, and I end up squirting all over her beautiful face. Kim is a champ and laps it up, taking every last drop and only loosening her grip on my ass when I start to lose my balance. The orgasm and squirting took too much from me, and I fall into the bed next to her. Kim smiles at me before heading to the bathroom to clean her face. My wetness is all over her, and the pillow she was using is soaked, too. I want to apologize, but she comes back and starts kissing me, her lips melting into mine. I can tell she's not mad about it at all. If anything, she looks like she's ready for round two—or would that be three?

EIGHT

Kim

I've never had a woman squirt on my face before, but I never want it to end. I knew Zara was about to orgasm, but when she came with a gush all over my face, I felt like I was in heaven. I couldn't taste her fast enough. Sure, we'd probably need to change the sheets and the pillowcases, but who cares? I want—no, need—more.

"I don't think I can come again right now," Zara whispers against my lips.

"Mmm, do you want me to stop?" I ask as I trail my fingers down her stomach.

"No, not at all."

Her eyes close and she relaxes under me. I notice the vibrator on the nightstand and get an idea. Maybe she isn't ready for another orgasm again right now, but I'm dying to explode. I reach over to grab the toy, still straddling Zara, and she peeks open her eyes to see what I'm doing. She raises an eyebrow before I turn it on and smile.

"Can I use this? I know you're not ready, but I could use another orgasm."

"Oh, fuck yes." Zara nods encouragingly.

I turn it to a medium setting and slip it between my thighs. I push the toy against my clit and moan. Zara props herself up on the pillows so she can watch. I've never been one to put on a show for someone else, but suddenly it feels invigorating. She watches me with bedroom eyes, her blues following my hands and then gliding up every inch of my body.

The buzzing fills the room as I rock my hips forward and let it press against my clit even harder. I gasp, feeling the intensity growing. I'm already a firecracker ready to explode just from getting Zara off. But touching myself, while she's naked underneath me? Pure heaven. She starts playing with her breasts, tugging at her nipples and squeezing her boobs. She bites down on her bottom lip, and I lean forward to suck on it. She groans into my mouth, and I whimper.

"Fuck, you turn me on so much," I admit.

I rock my hips against hers, and she moans.

"God, you feel so good." She whimpers.

I move the vibrator in small circles against my clit—until my breath hitches.

"Oh, fuck! I'm coming!" I scream and hold the toy against my clit until the orgasm rushes over me.

I try to hold eye contact with Zara, but I can't. My orgasm is so powerful that I close my eyes and fall back to the bed. I toss the toy aside, and before I can say anything, I feel Zara's mouth against my pussy.

"Oh, fuck!" I scream as she latches onto my clit. Her perfect lips are sucking and tightening, which makes me come all over again.

"Yes! Zara! Fuck me!" I scream out as loud as I can.

"God, you're so beautiful when you come," she whispers in my ear. She nibbles the lobe of my ear gently, and I have to try and catch my breath.

"Mmm." I kiss her lips softly, and she lies down next to me.

We're on the opposite end of the bed—with no pillows—but she holds out her arm for me and I tuck myself into her arms. She's warm and comfortable, and it's the exact thing I need right now. I don't want to be clingy, but I need *some* comfort after hooking up with someone. I trace my hands over her stomach, around the curves of her breasts, and down to her hip bones. I look at her body more than I have the last few times. It's hard to take in every detail of someone's body when you're having an orgasm.

"Do you have any tattoos?" I ask.

"Not yet, no."

"Really?" I can't hide the surprise in my voice.

"Yeah, I mean, I want them. I just never got around to it." Zara shrugs.

"Huh," I mumble.

"What?"

"You just seem like the type to have a tattoo."

"Well, you've seen every inch of me, so I think you can confirm I don't have any." She laughs. "I've never been able to decide on what I want."

"Ah, it took me years to figure out the ones I wanted. I never pull the trigger until I'm like, a million percent sure."

"We should go get tattoos," Zara says casually.

"Excuse me?" I sit up to look at her.

"What? I want one, I think it would be a fun experience. You said you've been doing things that scare you, right? So, come get a matching tattoo with a woman you barely know."

"What would we even get?" I can feel my heart racing just thinking about it.

"That's the fun of it, we won't decide until we get there." Zara smirks.

"W-what?"

"Come on, let's do it."

Zara stands and starts looking for her clothes. She puts on a fresh pair of panties and throws on a cotton sundress over it. I'm still sitting on the bed, staring at her in shock, while she looks for her phone.

"You're not being serious, right?"

"Haven't you ever done anything spontaneous?" Zara asks, leaning on the bed to put her face in front of mine.

"I mean, that's sort of how we ended up here."

"I know, and that's been good, right?" Zara waits for the answer she already knows.

"Of course."

"So, be spontaneous with me. We'll spend the summer fucking and doing things we thought we'd never do. Say yes!" Zara says it in a way that I don't feel any pressure. If I tell her no, I have no doubt she'd come back to bed and watch a movie or relax with me.

"Yes," I say without thinking about it.

"Yes!" Zara leans in and slips her tongue in my mouth. I kiss her for a moment before she pulls back.

"Shit, I cannot wear that dress to get a tattoo, my whole ass was out on the drive over."

"Borrow something of mine, we're probably the same size. Go for it." She opens her closet and suitcase full of clothes.

I peek through and grab a pair of jean shorts for under my dress and slip them over the lingerie I'm wearing. I'm not wearing panties, and that would probably not be the most comfortable choice later, but I'm not about to put my soaked thong back on. Nor am I going to borrow panties. That feels a little *too* intimate.

"Let's do this." I smile, and Zara holds the door open for me.

By the time we get to my car, I realize I have no idea where I'm going.

"Where are we going?"

"Is there a tattoo shop in town?" Zara asks, and I shake my head. We're lucky we have a bookstore. "Okay, my phone says there's one in Bloomington, that's the next town over, right? They're open until midnight."

"Perfect, pop in the address to the navigation app, and we'll go."

I start to drive, and I can feel my anxiety creeping up on me.

That's one of the worst things about having anxiety; it has a tendency to sneak up on you when you least expect it. I take a few deep breaths and remind myself I can back out at any time. Right now, I'm just driving. I can get through each step slowly. Zara squeezes my thigh, and I relax a bit.

We pull into the tattoo shop parking lot, and I read the sign: Hurricane Ink. I remind myself I can back out at any time, and I relax again. Zara looks more excited than I thought she'd be, and she's racing to hold the door open for me. The receptionist, who is covered in tattoos, greets us and asks us to check in.

"What can we do for you today?" she asks once she checks we're both over eighteen.

"We want to get tattoos, but we aren't sure on what we want. It's a little spontaneous."

"It's not like a romantic thing, right? Like you're thinking about getting each other's names or something?"

"No, nothing like that," I say quickly.

"Okay good. We don't do couple tattoos here. We constantly get requests to cover them up. It's not worth it." She grimaces. "We do have a 'get what you get' machine where you put in a coin and whatever you get, you get. You pull a random design, and we tattoo it. It's slightly cheaper and fun if you don't know what you want."

"Is there a hint of what can be inside?" I ask hopefully.

"Nope, but each is an actual design. No words or X-rated themes. Some are fun, but there's nothing inappropriate you'd have to cover up for work," she reassures me.

"Let's do it! Kim?" Zara looks at me. I want to say *no* but for some reason, with Zara smiling at me, I can't.

"Fuck it, let's do it." I throw caution to the wind and ignore my gut telling me no. I'm tired of being so damn predictable. I want to be fun.

"Okay, just fill out this form, and then we'll give you the coin for the machine. It'll be seventy-five dollars each."

"Here you go." Zara hands over a card, and I do the same.

We take our time filling out the forms. Then the receptionist hands us each a coin, and we walk to the machine.

"Why don't you get yours first, but then we can open them at the same time," Zara suggests.

"Sure." I plop the coin in and out rolls one of those small containers with a colorful lid. There's a folded-up paper inside, and I'm dying to see what it is as Zara puts her coin inside the machine. Hers rolls out, and then we both look at each other.

"Ready?" she asks, and I nod.

We crack open our containers and pull out the designs. Mine is a small red pepper with a green top. I glance at hers and realize she somehow got the same one. "No way!" I say with a laugh.

"Oh, my goodness! Now we definitely have to get them!" Zara smiles big.

"Fuck it, let's go!" I agree.

"Where do you want to get them?" the receptionist asks.

"My hip?" Zara shrugs.

"Hell, yeah. Me too."

"We should get them on opposite hips so when we stand next to each other we can take a picture," Zara suggests.

"Okay." I smile. I like the thought of having a piece of Zara on my body forever. She makes me feel wild, free—totally unlike the woman I once was.

We're led to the back of the shop, and two male tattoo artists introduce themselves as Pat and Bobby. They ask where we want the tattoos and if we'd like anything to protect our privacy since we're getting the tattoos on an intimate area. Zara declines but I take a blanket since I'm not wearing any panties. I unbutton my shorts just enough for the stencil to be placed, and I agree on the placement. I'm not nervous; I've had tattoos before. The Harry Styles quote on my ribs and the watermelon slice on my forearm. Both of which can be easily covered up at work. Not that I'm not allowed to have tattoos.

I watch Zara through the mirror as she lies down to get her

tattoo. My tattoo artist is sort of quiet, but I don't mind; it gives me a chance to study Zara. Her artist is chatty, and she's making him laugh. Her bright red lips curve upward as she teases him about something. It's too loud in here to hear what, but he's smiling too. If I didn't know better, I'd think they were flirting, and I have to ignore the feeling rolling in my stomach. Zara and I are temporary. I can't go and catch feelings for a relationship that has an expiration date.

NINE

Zara

"Tattoo reveal time!" I shout, jumping over to Kim's table.

She sits up and we both walk over to the mirror and show off our tiny tats. I snap a pic of our hips side by side before the artists call us back to tape them up. They put something called SecondSkin over our tattoos, and it's basically a clear sticker to protect the skin from infection. We're given the rundown of tattoo care, and then we're free to go. We tip our artists and then head back to Kim's car. She's sort of quiet, so I reach for her wrist as we make it to the car.

"What's going on in that head of yours?"

"I don't know. I thought I'd be anxious, but I surprisingly feel relaxed," she admits. I can tell the feeling is bothering her. Like maybe she's uncomfortable with being content.

"Want me to help you relax?" I ask. Kim raises an eyebrow, but before she can answer, I lean in to kiss her.

Pressing her body against mine, she drops the keys and her back hits the car door. I rock my hips carefully against hers and let our tongues explore. She relaxes under my touch, and I intertwine my fingers in hers as we kiss. We stay like this until a car pulls into the parking lot with its brights on. Pulling apart with a blush and my lipstick smudged on her lips, I bend to get her keys. I hand them to her and head to the other side of the car.

"Can you put in the address for the Inn?" Kim asks, and I nod.

She starts to drive, and I flip down the passenger side mirror to fix my lipstick. I pull the tube out of my purse, pucker my lips, and reapply it. When I'm done, I look over at Kim and she slides her gaze to me for just a second.

"What? Did I miss a spot?" I'm about to pull down the mirror again when Kim whips the car into a random empty parking lot.

"Where—" I'm about to ask but Kim kisses me as she shifts the car into park. The kiss is hard and passionate, like she *needs* to have me right now.

"You look so freaking hot with that lipstick. I just needed to kiss you right now," she explains between neck kisses.

I tilt my head back and moan as she starts to suck on my neck. Is she giving me a hickey? I forgot they even exist. Her hand goes for my boob, and I tangle my hands in her hair. I feel like a fucking teenager making out in some abandoned parking lot. I can't remember the last time kissing someone just for the sake of kissing was this much fun. It's like Kim's lips were made for me.

"Let's get in the backseat," Kim mumbles against me.

"Fuck it."

She climbs in the back after making sure the car is off. Then I climb over, almost falling on her and landing on the seat next to her—so graceful. Her car is immaculate, so we don't have to move anything. She pulls me back in and kisses me. Kim climbs on my lap, and I grab her ass under her shorts. She grinds on me slowly, and I kiss her neck this time. I suck harder than she did, wanting to leave my mark on her. With her head tossed back in the moonlight, she looks like a goddess. I'm about to slide my hands up her dress when a bright light appears at the window and a knock follows suit.

"Oh, fuck," Kim mumbles, quickly getting off my lap.

Inn Love

She opens the window with the window crank in the back and grimaces as she faces the police officer in front of us. At least, I think it's a cop—until I read his oversized hat that tells me he's actually a state trooper. Is that like, a small-town cop? I really should make note of that for my book. But now is not the time to be thinking about that.

"Evening, ladies. I'm not going to ask what's going on here, but you can't be parked in this lot. I'm going to need you to move your car and head on home." He has a thick Northeast accent and a mustache. At first, I can't tell why he looks so familiar, but then I realize it—he looks like Bella's dad in *Twilight*.

"Sorry, officer. No problem," Kim chirps.

"You two haven't been drinking, right?" He glances between us, like he could tell by looking at us.

"No, sir." Kim smiles.

"We were just celebrating, sir. I just got a job offer that we're very excited about, and we wanted to memorialize the moment. I apologize," I add for good measure. It's a total lie, but the trooper softens at my story.

"Well, congratulations. Now I need to see you head to the front seat and get on home." He holds the door open for us and Kim gets out first, heading to the driver's side.

It's like a walk of shame as the officer stands back to watch us get in. He only starts walking to his car when he sees Kim put the keys in. Once we're back on the highway toward Lovers, I burst out laughing. At first, Kim looks at me like I'm nuts, and then she bursts out with laughter too.

"Oh, my goodness! I thought we were about to get arrested for kissing in the back of the car!" Kim exclaims.

"Well, someone just *had* to have me," I tease.

"I was trying to be spontaneous! See where that got me." Her cheeks are a dark red color. Even in the moonlight, I can tell.

"I liked it." I shrug.

"Until we got caught! And you lied! To a police officer!"

"Eh, who cares?" I say with a shrug. "Also, technically it was a state trooper."

Kim and I start laughing, and we don't stop until we make it back to the Inn. Kim pulls into a parking spot and then pauses. We never really talked about how the night would end, but I don't want it to. I know I'll be seeing her again; we've talked about it more than once. But I'm not sure I want to wait that long.

"Wanna stay over tonight?"

"Really?"

"Yeah, I mean it's late, and we're having fun. Why not continue it?" I shrug like it's not a big deal. I don't want her to feel pressured, but I also really want her to say yes.

"Okay, but can I take a shower?"

"Only if I can join you." I wink.

We head inside the Inn. At night, Miss Taylor locks the front door, so I use the key to let myself in. I appreciate the extra lock at night. I know Lovers is a far cry from NYC, but murders can happen anywhere. Kim follows me upstairs, and we both get undressed, tossing our clothes to the side. I turn on the hot water and let it warm up. We both get in, and although Kim looks sexy as hell and all I want to do is fuck her again, we both agree we're too exhausted to have sex tonight. Instead, we both get clean and head to bed for the night.

I lend Kim a brush and an extra-large sleep T-shirt. "I can give you this, but I don't wear pajamas to bed."

"That's fine with me. My boobs get too chilly if I don't wear something," she says with a smile.

"I actually love that." I laugh.

I climb into bed and turn on the TV. Kim finishes brushing her hair and climbs into bed next to me. We've tossed aside the wet pillow from earlier and pulled out a fresh one from the closet. I hope I won't have to explain that one to Miss Taylor. I'm sure she's seen worse around here.

"So, what made you want to teach Kindergarten?" I ask Kim.

"Well, I really love kids. I'm not sure that I want to have any of my own, but I love them for short amounts of time. And Kindergarten age is perfect because they're still cute, but you can teach them stuff. And they say a lot of out-of-pocket things and have a unique perspective on life."

"You don't want kids?" I ask, realizing that's probably the one part of her answer I shouldn't have focused on.

"Not really. I mean, kids are cool, but I've never seen myself having them. My friends all want them, and I can see them being great parents, but I'd be content being the cool aunt. Pop in to say hi and then leave." Kim shrugs.

"That makes sense. I have five sisters, and they all have kids. They kind of look at me like I'm nuts when I say I don't want kids."

"Oh, yeah. Some people are super judgmental about that. But I've also seen what happens when people who don't want kids have them. The kid is usually miserable."

"Is that from experience, or?"

"No, no. My parents are great! I've seen it with kids in my class. So neglected and sad. I feel bad for them." She sighs.

"I'm sorry. I didn't mean for it to get so deep." I chuckle awkwardly.

"No worries. So, five sisters? Where are you in the lineup? Oldest?"

"You don't see me as the youngest?" I tease.

"I mean, maybe? Actually, no. You have a caretaking vibe about you that usually comes from being an older sibling."

"I'm the third oldest, so I'm sort of in the middle." I smile. It feels nice that Kim just seems to *get* me.

"Was it chaos growing up with so many siblings?"

"Sort of. We're all very close, although we're spread out all over the country now. We were born and raised in New York, but they sort of all took off in different directions. My little sister,

Ruby, is the only one who lives nearby. She's in East Village and I'm in SoHo."

"Do you see them often?"

"We see each other on holidays. Sometimes it's someone's house, sometimes it's a place we've all wanted to go."

"That's so fun. My parents just moved out of our childhood home into something smaller, and they never vacation—ever."

"Do you like to travel?"

"I don't even have a passport."

"If you could go anywhere, where would it be?"

Kim pauses for a long moment to think about it. Her eyes squint, and she focuses on something in her head while she contemplates my question.

"I'd love to go to Australia. The beaches, the vibes, the accents. I just feel like I'd have so much fun."

"What's stopping you from going?"

"Besides the funds?" She laughs. "I don't know. It just seems so far to go by myself."

"I think there's a lot of stigma around it, but I travel around a lot by myself, and I love it. No one to make you late or make silly stops. You can do whatever you want on your own time."

"Now that you put it like that..."

"Tell me you'll travel, maybe not to Australia right away, but that you'll travel alone at least once."

"Okay. I will." Kim smiles, and I look into her eyes. We hold each other's gaze for longer than two friends should, until Kim looks away with a blush.

"We should get some sleep," Kim says with a yawn.

"Okay." I nod.

We decide to leave the TV on, which I'm thankful for because I can't sleep. Kim's out in minutes, but my mind is racing. I've never felt like this with someone else before. Sure, I've had relationships, but they never felt like this. Maybe that's because this is so clearly *not* a relationship? Kim and I will be going our separate ways at the end of the summer, and I'll have nothing more than this tattoo and some heartbreak to remember her by. Still, I think it might be worth it. Having my heart broken by Kim is better than having none of her at all.

TEN

Kim

I wake up in the morning feeling a little disoriented. I'm still not used to sleeping in my apartment yet. But when I slowly open my eyes, I realize I'm not in my new apartment. I spent the night at Zara's hotel room. She's peacefully sleeping next to me, her mouth wide open with a little bit of drool dripping onto her pillow. I smile. She's so cute. I toss back the sheets and sneak into the bathroom to relieve myself. I wash my hands and steal a swipe of toothpaste on my finger just so I don't have morning breath. Then, I retie my hair into a bun and climb back into bed. Zara wakes with the movement of the bed and smiles.

"Hey, good morning." She yawns.

"Hi." I settle into my spot as Zara wipes her mouth dry.

"Oh, my god, was I drooling?" She laughs.

"Yes, you were."

"Damn, I try to impress the pretty girl in my bed, and instead, I drool everywhere."

"It was sort of cute," I admit.

"No freaking way. Wait, do you always look like that when you wake in the morning? Because that is seriously unfair."

"I just got up a few minutes ago, and I brushed my teeth. It's not like I put on makeup or anything." I giggle.

"Well, then that's really rude. I'm afraid you have to go make yourself look ugly so I can feel better about my drool situation."

"Oh, stop it." I playfully shove her shoulder.

"You stop it." She playfully shoves me back.

When I go to do it again, she grabs my hand and props it over my head. In one swift movement, she climbs over me and straddles my hips. I wince, a soreness I didn't expect flaring up, and for a brief second, I'm confused. Until I remember the tattoos we got last night.

"Sorry, is your tattoo sensitive? I can get down." Zara goes to move, but I stop her by holding her hips still.

"I'm good like this."

Zara dips down to kiss me, and I moan against her lips. Her bare body presses against the cotton T-shirt, but I feel every inch of her. Her pussy is positioned over my thigh, and her desire is growing. I slide a finger between her legs letting the wetness coat my fingers.

"Mmm," she whimpers.

"Get down on your knees," I command.

Zara's eyes light up, and she throws back the sheets, dropping to her knees on the carpet. I slide my body to the side and lean my butt against the bed. I throw off my T-shirt, and Zara bites her lip in anticipation.

"I want you to make me come."

Zara wastes no time before latching onto my pussy. I grab her blonde curls, gripping them tightly as her nose brushes against my clit. I'm still sensitive from the last time we were intimate. She reaches up to touch my breast and play with my nipple, lightly tugging and flicking with her fingers while she tastes me.

"Oh, yes!" I cry out.

Her tongue isn't following any sort of pattern; she moves as if she's ravenous for me. I can't take it. I look down and see her blue eyes staring back at me. Her cheeks turn upward, as if she's

Inn Love

smiling, but her face is buried in my pussy. I grind my hips against her, begging for more. God, this is the best way to wake up. This might be the most sex I've ever had in my life. It isn't like I never had sex with my exes, but this fiery passion? The two of us unable to keep our hands off each other? I've never had that before.

"Yes! Right there!" I call out as Zara uses her finger inside me.

My orgasm begs to be let free. I hold eye contact with her, wanting to see her and commit this to memory. I'll be thinking about this forever. Her blonde hair in my fingers, her eyes deep with desire as she looks at me. *Fuck.*

"I'm coming! I'm coming!" I scream as I fall backward into the bed. Zara keeps going for a moment or two until I catch my breath. Then she slaps my clit, not hard but with every nerve heightened, I whimper.

"God, that was the perfect way to start my day. I am not a morning person at all." Zara laughs. She gives me a bottle of water and waits for me to take a sip. I've noticed that's kind of her thing, making sure I always drink after an orgasm. It's sweet.

"I'm a morning person if I have coffee but apparently orgasms work too." I laugh.

Zara hops into bed next to me and we kiss for a bit. Once I gain my strength, I make her come for me—twice. Out of breath, we lie back on the pillows.

"What are you up to today?" I ask but then realize it might sound like I'm asking to stay longer, and I get anxious.

"I've been spending my days exploring the town and writing. I see different places, take different paths, and then find somewhere to write. It's usually the café because it's cute and quiet. What about you?"

"I have to unpack some boxes in my apartment. I've been putting it off, and it's really bugging me."

"When did you move back?" Zara asks.

"Just a few weeks ago." I pause before offering. "Do you

want a ride into town? I can drop you off somewhere if you don't wanna walk."

"That's okay. It's probably the New Yorker in me, but I like long walks. It's part of the adventure."

"Okay." I climb out of bed and look for my clothes.

I put on the wrap dress and decide to carry the lingerie. It's a pain in the ass to put back on, and I don't know where my thong is. I look like a walk of shame AD, but it isn't like anyone I know is going to see me here.

"I'm gonna get more sleep before I start my day, but let me walk you out." Zara's getting dressed before I can protest.

She follows me downstairs, and when we get to the front door, she stops to kiss me.

"I had fun. Let's plan something soon?" She asks.

"Or maybe we'll be spontaneous and be at the same place again?"

"Sounds perfect to me." Zara kisses me again before I head to my car.

I can feel the fresh air on my ass, but in a way, it sort of feels nice. Heading to my apartment, I wish I could stop for some coffee, but no way am I going anywhere in town with no panties on. I'll have to settle for my Keurig machine coffee; thankfully I know where the pods are. When I get inside, the first thing I do is change into comfortable clothes—a pair of leggings and an oversized T-shirt. I toss the lingerie in the laundry basket and make a note on my to-do list to buy more. I've always like picking out lingerie and dressing up, but none of my exes ever seemed into it. Of course, Zara is the exception to that. The way she lit up when she saw me and how turned on she was...? That's worth my cold ass and lost thong.

I make a cup of coffee and turn on the air conditioning. I didn't close the blinds before I left yesterday, and the sun is shining in, so it's warm in here. I sip my coffee as I go around closing each set of blinds and curtains. Then I pick a box and drag it to the coffee table to start unpacking.

Inn Love

I actually enjoy unpacking; it's mindless, and I love choosing a place for everything. I don't have pets or kids, so I can put the breakables wherever I want. My special edition Harry Styles records already have a special shelf over the TV in the living room. Most of my stuff is a small nod to him. A lot of it is subtle, and normal people wouldn't pick up on them without knowing things about him or his music. Like my poster in the kitchen, which is a drawing of pancakes for two people, a bottle of maple syrup, hashbrowns, egg yolks, and the words, *I will always love you*.

The air cools the place down fairly quickly, so I lower the fan and finish my coffee. I had the place repainted before I moved in. Each room is a different color, but everything is in muted tones. I wanted the place to be fun but not too over the top. My bedroom is my favorite: a light pink that lights up the room. I have splashes of color on my bedspread and curtains with all white furniture. It makes the place seem even bigger. It's a miracle I even found this place. I'd been looking for months—ever since Billy and I broke up. The last thing I wanted to do was keep sharing a place with him. The second we broke up, I applied to the job at Lover's Elementary, and as soon as I was accepted, I started my apartment hunt. An old friend of my mother's got me this place because she was heading to Florida for her retirement. She wanted someone responsible to rent her space out to—and she didn't mind that I wanted to transform it, so it's a win-win.

As I unpack another box of records, I decide to put one on. I, of course, pick a Harry Styles album and relax as I hum along to the familiar tune. I can't sing for my life, and I don't really like to. I prefer leaving it to the professionals. It's like when you go to a concert and take videos, but then all you can hear is yourself singing back. It's such a pet peeve of mine.

I finish another box and take a seat to give myself a break. I only have...seven more boxes in this room. There are about three more in my bedroom, and then I'll officially be done unpacking.

Maybe once I'm done, I can have Zara over. We did say we'd

hang out again, we're friends with benefits, after all. I'd love to have the chance to fuck her in my own bed. I live in an apartment with two other tenants above me, so maybe we'd have to be quiet. That won't be a problem for me, and it might be fun to have to keep Zara from screaming.

I can picture it now, her body writhing, begging for me to let her come and me stopping every time she got too loud. She'd be so mad yet so freaking turned on. I open my eyes and shake it off. I shouldn't be this horny; I orgasmed only hours ago—and I came more than once. Zara is definitely doing something to me. The more I'm with her, the more I'm craving her.

I wish it wasn't too soon to call her. I'd ask her to come over and hang out tonight. I don't want to seem like a clingy girlfriend, though. I know where we stand. We just spent most of the last twenty-four hours with together, and I'm already missing her. This is supposed to be casual. I can do casual, right?

No. Probably not, since anything I've ever had that was somewhat friendly turned into a serious relationship.

Still, I know what this is. At least, that's what I'll keep telling myself. Zara lives in New York, and she hates small towns. She isn't going to magically decide to move here when summer's over. I have a few weeks left with her, and that's it. My heart aches at the thought. I know I probably shouldn't be putting myself through this. I don't need to start the school year with a heartbreak.

At the same time, I also know there's nothing that'll keep me from seeing Zara.

ELEVEN

Zara

"Are you sure you don't mind taking Sandy with you?" Miss Taylor makes a face.

"I'd love to. I made a friend here and she loves dogs, so I thought it might be fun. I know you mentioned how Sandy loves swimming."

"Hmm," she says, hesitating.

"I can give her a bath, too, if that's what you're worried about."

"Oh no, it's fine. Come on Sandy! You can go play with Zara today!" Miss Taylor calls her over, and Sandy comes running.

"We'll be back later." I smile and take Sandy's leash.

I'm meeting Kim at the beach today. I took a tour of the lighthouse last week, but I want to go swimming near it, too. It seems like a small-town to do. Kim insisted on bringing lunch, and I said I'd bring Sandy along. I think she's more excited to see the dog than me, but I don't take it too personally.

"Zara!" Kim calls as Sandy and I make our way down the beach.

Kim's already there with a blanket spread out and a big umbrella to block the sun. She's wearing a bright pink bikini top that's tied like a bow in the front. She's paired it with cropped floral bottoms. She waves us over, and Sandy goes running toward her. Kim kneels to pet Sandy, but the dog is so excited to see her that she licks her face and knocks her back.

"Sandy!" I catch up to her and pull her off Kim, who's laughing it off. "I'm sorry."

"Don't be, she's just saying hi." Kim stands up and shakes the sand off herself.

"It's nice to see you." I smile.

I want to lean in to kiss her, but I'm not sure what the protocol is. We aren't dating, and normally I wouldn't think twice about it, but for some reason I'm hesitant. We're in public, and it's a small town. I don't know if she wants to be seen kissing someone, let alone kissing someone she isn't committed to. Is she seeing other people? We never really talked about that, and although I have no right to be jealous, I definitely am. I want to be the only one making her come.

"It's so nice out today; it's just hot enough to not be sweltering." Kim smiles.

I take off my cover-up and reveal my one-piece bathing suit. It's split in three spots, one on each side of my ribs and one in the back. I take a seat next to her on the sheet and set down my stuff. Sandy happily basks in the sun, lying on her back with her tongue hanging out. Kim watches me as I slide on my sunglasses and pull out a bottle of water.

"Do you want anything to eat?"

"You didn't have to pack lunch. I could've brought something."

"I'm gluten-free, so it sort of makes it complicated if I don't do it. I don't like to risk contamination if I'm not the one to make it."

"You're gluten-free? How did I not know that?"

"It hasn't really come up yet." She shrugs. "It's no big deal."

"Are you, like, allergic? Or is it just a dietary choice?"

"I have celiac disease, which is manageable. I just can't

directly have gluten, or I get sick. It won't kill me. It just hurts my stomach."

"Gotcha." I nod. I'm glad I didn't accidentally give her gluten without knowing it.

"I brought a ton of fruit, and some turkey wraps and chips." She opens the bag, and I peek in.

"Wow, you went all out."

"I like to be prepared."

"I'm good for now, but I'll definitely steal something later," I assure her.

"Do you swim?"

"Oh, yes. I don't get of a lot of opportunity in the city, but I love it."

"Me too! My friends and I used to live at the beach all summer."

"Are you all still close?"

"Yeah. They're my best friends. One of them is getting married at the end of the summer, so the rest of the gang is back for prep and events. I'm supposed to see them tomorrow night, actually."

"That's awesome. How many are in your friend group?"

"Five of us. Heather, Ryleigh, Norah, Alana, and me. Plus, Alana's little sister Wrenn sometimes joins us, and Alana's college roommate is the maid of honor, so she's probably coming along too."

"That's awesome. Are you excited for the wedding?"

"Not really." Kim grimaces, and I laugh out loud. I love how transparent she is.

"Why's that?"

"I just...I don't know. I kind of hate weddings. There's so much prep and fuss just for one day. It seems like a lot of work."

"Do you have to wear a silly bridesmaid dress?"

"Thankfully no. She picked out really tasteful and flattering dresses."

"Can I see?"

"I don't think I have a picture, actually. I'll have to take one..." Kim stops herself from finishing her sentence, but I know what she was going to say. She'd send me one at the wedding, but since the wedding is at the end of the summer, who knows if I'll still be here. And who knows if we'll even stay in contact after that.

The silence lingers between us for a few moments. There's too much unsaid between us. I don't have the words to make it right, so I change the subject.

"Want to go for a swim?"

"I'd love to." Kim smiles.

"Come on Sandy, let's go swim!" I tell Sandy, and she takes off for the water.

I stand and hold out my hand for Kim, she takes it, and we walk toward the water. It's cool on my toes, but it quickly warms up. We both decide to dive in headfirst to take the brunt of it. Kim flips her hair back, dark curls cascading down her back. I keep an eye on Sandy so she doesn't go out too far. I assume she knows what to do, but I don't exactly know how to save a dog from currents. Do they have special dog lifeguards? Fuck, I don't think they even have regular lifeguards here. But Sandy is sticking close to us, doggy paddling in the water and having a grand old time.

"Can we play with your dog?" a group of three kids ask, swimming over to us.

"Sure, her name is Sandy." I smile. I have no idea how old these kids are, but they look young enough to stay close to shore. Plus, they have a ball—how could I tell Sandy no to that?

"Come on Sandy!" the little girl calls, and the dog accidentally splashes her while trying to get closer.

I swim over to Kim and slip my hands on her waist, but she tenses. I immediately pull back, not wanting to make her uncomfortable.

"Are you okay?"

"I— I just. I'm not the biggest fan of PDA if this isn't a relationship. I don't exactly know who's in my class yet, and I don't want rumors of me and a beautiful woman to spin around the school. Not because I'm not out, but because I like to keep my private life at school private," Kim explains.

"Of course. That completely makes sense." I wish I could touch her and kiss her, but she wants to be professional. I respect that.

We swim for a bit, keeping an eye on Sandy and the kids. The adult they came with sits on the beach. She waves at us when we look around. She's lounging with a magazine in hand and clearly no intention of coming in the water. I think she's thankful for Sandy because she's keeping the kids busy.

We eventually grow tired of swimming and head up to the shore. We let the kids know where we'll be and ask them to bring Sandy in when they get tired of swimming. I'm still keeping an eye on her because I refuse to leave her in the hands of three unknown kids. Especially if, all of a sudden, Sandy chooses not to listen to them.

"Do you need more sunblock?" I ask Kim. She's tanned all over, but anyone can burn.

"I do, actually. Thank you." She takes the spray from me and stands a few feet from the blanket so she can spray herself. I do the same and toss the bottle into my bag. I'm pale as a ghost, and I need to reapply every hour, or I'll be a lobster.

"Want something to eat?" Kim takes out a sandwich for herself, and I take some fruit.

It's a mix of pineapple, strawberries, and grapes. It looks delicious and juicy. Kim starts eating, and I glance at Sandy with the kids. They're still playing, and the lighthouse in the background makes the setting look like a Norman Rockwell painting. Small towns are different, that's for sure. Everyone is so nice and so open. No one seems to be afraid that I might kidnap or murder their kids.

I grew up in Queens—a place where you steer clear of strangers unless you're lost, and even then, it's still ill-advised.

"We have to go home, but thanks for letting us play with Sandy." One of the kids come by, dripping wet, with Sandy next to him.

"You're welcome. Thanks for keeping her busy. Have a great day." I smile.

Sandy smiles and shakes off her whole body, getting water and sand everywhere.

"Sandy!" I yell. I know she can't help it, but I hate when dogs do that.

"Oh, shit. I think I got sand in my eye." Kim holds one eye shut and tries blinking.

"Crap, can you open it?" I put down the food I'm holding and look for a bottle of water.

"Not really. Ugh, yeah, there's definitely something in there." She winces.

"Okay, I need you to hold your head back, and I'll pour some water over your eye. Then blink like a crazy person to flush it out," I explain, crawling over to her.

"Okay." She's frowning, and there are tears cascading down her cheeks.

I pour the water and hold her face steady so she doesn't flinch. The water's colder than I want it to be, but it's all we have. She blinks really fast and then opens her eye. The whites of her eyes have turned a bit red, but I don't see anything.

"You okay?"

"Yes, thank you. That really hurt." She blinks and tries to get her eye back to normal.

"It might hurt for a bit, but at least you got it out."

I let go of her face, but I don't move away. My face is only inches from hers as I look deep into her eyes. She blushes and I smile. My eyes drop to her lips, and I can see her breath catch when she notices. She looks like a woman who wants to be kissed. I want to kiss her, but I also know how she feels about PDA, so I want to be respectful. I pull away and sit back down on the blanket. Sandy lies down between us, and I try to ignore the fact that my feelings for her are more than friendly.

TWELVE

Kim

Zara is in front of me, and instead of letting her pull away, I lean in to kiss her. Who cares about PDA and what people might think? All I want are her lips on mine. Everything around us fades to black. Her hands rake through my curls, and I hold her waist against mine. I can feel the smoothness of her skin and the fabric of her silky bathing suit. She moans into my mouth, and I rock my hips against hers. All I want is to take her back to the hotel room and have my way with her but—

"Are you even listening?" Alana snaps in front of my face.

"What?" I blush. Everyone is looking at me, and it's clear they know I was in another world.

"Oh my gosh, are you blushing!?" Heather squeals.

"Who were you thinking about?" Ryleigh asks with a smile.

"Nothing, no one," I lie. I pick up my drink and take a hearty sip.

"Are you seeing someone?" Alana raises a dark eyebrow at me, and I avoid eye contact.

"She doesn't have to spill if she's not ready," Norah adds, and I send her a thankful smile.

"Anyway! I was saying thank you for all your help today. I

was stressed out of my mind but you all really helped me through." Alana raises a glass for a toast.

We all clink glasses, and I take a sip of my drink. I absolutely hate it. It's a whiskey sour, and I think they should be illegal. It's warm going down, and the sour mix makes the drink taste like I'm sucking on a lemon. But I went out of my comfort zone to order one, so I'm going to finish it—and then never order another one ever again. I wince as I suck down the last of it and step away from the group to order something else.

"Can I have something with vodka this time? I don't like whiskey." I grimace, handing Wrenn the glass.

"You got it." She smiles and disappears down the bar to make me something else.

"So, are you going to tell me about this mystery person?" Ryleigh comes up behind me.

She'd been so preoccupied with Wrenn the last few times we talked and texted that I haven't had the chance to tell her about Zara. Besides, I'm not even sure what to say. My one-night stand turned into friends with benefits. I want to say that's all there is to it, but I'm starting to fall for her, and I won't be able to hide that from Ryleigh.

"Her name is Zara."

"Like the author Norah is obsessed with?"

"What?"

"She said this famous romance author came into the store last week. She was fangirling and everything. I'm surprised she didn't tell you."

"What's the author's name?"

"Zara Low? Lamb? No! Lee! Zara Lee!"

I pull out my phone and search the name on Instagram. Immediately, the profile pops up and Norah is following it. Holy shit. It's Zara. She has over 100,000 followers. She completely downplayed how famous she is.

"Is that her? She's hot." Ryleigh glances over my shoulder.

"Who's hot?" Wrenn crosses her arms after handing me my drink.

"The girl Kim's seeing," Ryleigh says, and Wrenn relaxes for a second.

"I'm not *seeing* her; we're just friends with benefits."

"You're just hooking up with someone?!" Ryleigh exclaims a little too loudly for my taste.

"Dude! We're in a small-town bar, can you keep it down?" I shoot her a look and she laughs.

"I'm just shocked. I didn't know you could do that. Like, have no feelings and do that."

"Well…"

"Oh, no. Let me guess. You caught feelings?" Ryleigh shakes her head.

"I just…it was supposed to be a one-night stand. But then she asked to see me again…"

"How did she find you?! You're supposed to leave no information and cut ties."

"She ran into me. She's staying at Harbor Inn for the summer," I explain.

"Ah, fuck. Okay, so now you're in love with her?"

"No! I just, I don't know. I just like being with her." I shrug.

"Does she feel the same?"

"I have no freaking clue."

We're both quiet, so we walk back to the group and I sip my new drink. I can't tell what's in it, except the vodka, but I like it. It doesn't burn my throat or make my lips pucker. I probably finish it too quickly, but soon, I'm ordering another one.

"We should dance!" Heather suggests. She's standing with a drink in her hand, her pink curls cascading down her back while she sways her hips.

"I don't think so." Alana and Norah shake their heads.

"Come on." Heather groans.

Ryleigh pounds down her beer and jumps up to join Heather.

"Yay!" Just before they're about to walk away, I call out after them. *Wait, was that me?*

"I wanna dance!" I finish my next drink and join them.

They all cheer, and we head for the jukebox. It's a million years old and sometimes doesn't work, but if you hit it on the side, it'll play for you. Heather puts a dollar in and plays some song I don't recognize, but it's got a nice beat. We all stand in a line and try to do the same thing but we're not sure who's leading who. And we're all way too drunk to try and be coordinated right now. So instead, we're all dancing on our own and laughing hysterically. We probably look like a bunch of drink idiots, but we were having fun.

I shake my head as I dance, and my hair is a mess. I close my eyes, and I can feel the beat of the music in my feet. I can't remember the last time I was drunk, let alone letting lose like this. My friends take my hands, and we belt out the words to a 2000s song. I can't help the smile on my face. Norah and Alana are smiling at us from afar. They might not be dancing with us, but I know they're not judging us either. That's the best part of this group. We may be different, we may change over the years, but we've always been here for each other, and we never judge. I feel safe with them, and I know I always will.

"Shots?!" I cheer and look at Heather and Ryleigh.

"Fuck, yes!" Heather yells, and they both nod.

We race to the bar, and Wrenn laughs as we each struggle to get on the stools. Why is it so freaking complicated to sit down? The leather on the stool is too slippery with my shorts, and I can't figure it out. I settle for standing while Wrenn pours out the shots of vodka.

"Cheers!" we all yell and toss them back.

This one has a bit more bite than before, and there's an aftertaste of peaches.

"Come on!" I take my friends hands.

This time, Alana and Norah join us. They aren't as drunk as we are, so they aren't going as hard with the dancing. It's still fun to have everyone here. I'm dancing for a bit when I realize I have to pee. I excuse myself and stumble toward the bathroom. It isn't that I'm wasted, it's just that when you try to walk in a line after dancing it's a little more difficult than you'd expect. I make it in, and I'm thankful there are multiple stalls because I suddenly *really* have to go.

I undo my zipper and sit down, letting out way more pee than I anticipated. I'm about to flush when I hear someone in the next stall crying. I peek down below and see a pair of pink heels and bare legs. There's no one else in the bathroom, and I'm not sure what to do. I stand up, getting a head rush as I pull up my shorts. You never realize how drunk you are until you sit down and get back up. I flush and unlock the door. I decide to give her a minute. I'll wash my hands, and if she's still crying when I'm done, I'll check on her.

I sing a song in my head about handwashing—the same one I teach my kindergarteners, and then I dry them completely. She's still crying, so I walk over to the stall and knock lightly. The crying stops as she sniffles.

"Hello? Are you okay in there?" I ask quietly.

"I-I'm fine." She sobs.

"I know you don't know me, but we can talk, if you'd like. I'm a good listener, and I'm pretty sure I won't remember this tomorrow."

She laughs. At least I'm making headway. She unlocks the door and walks out with tissue in her hands and her makeup running down her cheeks. She looks in the mirror and starts crying more.

"It's okay. I know it looks bad, but you can get the makeup off easy." I pick up some paper towels and wet them before handing them to her.

"Thanks." She sniffles.

"I'm Kim." I realize I never introduced myself.

"I'm Sasha." She wipes off clumps of mascara and pink eyeshadow.

"Are you here by yourself?" I ask, and apparently that's the wrong thing because she starts sobbing again.

"I'm sorry!" I say quickly.

"It's okay. I...Yeah, I am. My b-boyfriend brought me here... to break up with me, apparently. Then he left," she says, managing to get out the words between sobs.

"You're kidding me." I shake my head. Why are men the worst sometimes? Women suck sometimes, but they'd never do shit like this.

"No. I stupidly thought he was taking me out for my birthday, that's why I'm so dressed up." She motions to her bright pink sparkly dress and heels.

"Today's your birthday?" My jaw drops.

"Not today. It was last Saturday, but he forgot. I thought he was making it up to me. But instead, he brought me here to dump me. He thought I wouldn't make a scene if we were in public." She scoffs.

"What a dick," I mutter.

Sasha laughs. "You're right. What a dick."

"Look, I don't know him—or you—but you're way too pretty to be crying over a mediocre man. You can definitely do better. I've never met anyone who cries as pretty as you do." I'm probably saying way too much, but drunk Kim is chatty.

"Thank you, you don't have to say that."

"I'm serious! You have a gorgeous face, even with makeup all over it. And you're dressed like Margo Robbie on the *Barbie* tour. Anyone would be lucky to go out with you." I smile and brush some of her blonde hair from out of her face.

Sasha closes her eyes and leans in, and I do too. But at the last second, I pull back and awkwardly cough.

"I'm so sorry! You were being nice, I'm such an idiot." She looks like she's about to cry again.

"I was, and if I wasn't sort of seeing someone, I'd be more than flattered. But I'm sort of taken. I'm sorry." I frown.

I knew I could've kissed Sasha, and it wouldn't have bothered Zara. I mean, it couldn't have. We have a pact. Until the end of the summer. I can do whatever I want. But it still feels wrong.

"You really think I can do better?" Sasha whispers, looking in the mirror.

"Oh, yes. Don't settle for a man who can't even remember your birthday." I rub her shoulder and head back into the bar.

I don't know how long I was gone, or if my friends even noticed I was gone. Time is weird when you're drunk.

THIRTEEN

Zara

"That sounds like shit," I mutter to myself. It's after one a.m., and I have a feeling that anything I write is going to sound like shit, but here I am.

My best writing usually comes in the wee hours of the night. I slept half the day, grabbed takeout, and rushed back to get writing. I've been sitting all over this room. At the desk, the couch, and now I'm in the bed. I have to switch positions every so often or I get stiff. I stuff a barbecue chip in my mouth and take a swig of Diet Coke. When I'm on deadline, I eat like shit. It doesn't matter the rest of the time, but when I'm writing, like really writing, I just snack. I need a variety of salty and sweet snacks—but always Diet Coke. It isn't like I could have groceries delivered here in the middle of the night, so I grabbed a few bottles during the day and stuck them in the small fridge under the desk.

I finally cracked the first several chapters of the book. Ever since Kim came along, the words have been flying out of me again. I know it isn't a coincidence. I'm not going to tell Haley that, though. She would be too happy to rub that in my face. So instead, I've thrown myself into this draft. All I want to do is write and write until I'm done with this. I'm having trouble with the first sex scene. I don't know how I want it to be, and no matter how I position them, it comes out wrong. No pun intended. I can't tell if I want them to meet as strangers or if she knew he was stalking her. It's complicated.

I'm about to give up for the night when I hear a banging on my door. I slide my computer to the side and put on one of the cotton robes hanging on the bathroom door. Is Miss Taylor up this late? It isn't like anything else in this town is open late. Trust me, I looked not too long ago. I'm dying for more food, but I'll be roughing it with the snacks for tonight. I peek through the peephole and squint. I see a mess of brown hair, and then I see Kim dancing in the hallway. I think she's talking, too, but I can't hear her too well.

"Kim?" I open the door and her face lights up.

"Zara!" She wraps her arms around me, and I usher her inside.

I stop to look down the hall, making sure she's alone. She's never come over like this before, but maybe she's attempting to surprise me again? Do something out of her comfort zone? I take a look at her, and I quickly realize she's drunk off her ass.

"Are you drunk?" I ask, raising an eyebrow.

"Only a lot." She giggles and burps. Drunk Kim might be my favorite.

"And how did you get here?" I know she'd never drive drunk, but I also know the only Uber driver around.

"I hitched a ride with my friend's fiancé. He doesn't talk much, so I convinced him to drop me here. Alana was sleeping. Shhh." Kim laughs and shakes her body like she's going to dance.

"Okay, and you were out with your friends?" I ask, trying to piece together the night for her.

"Yup! We went to Teddy's! It's bar in town, and I had a lot of shots! Plus, this really gross whiskey drink. I think it was a whiskey sweet, but it was not sweet at all." She makes a face like she just sucked on a lemon.

"Do you mean a whiskey sour?" I ask, choking back a laugh.
"Yes! Do you like those? It was so icky."
"Not really, why did you have one?"
"I was trying new drinks, but I *definitely* do not like whiskey."

I shrug off the robe, starting to get hot with it on. Kim wastes no time looking my body over, and I blush. She's never usually this forward but her inhibitions are down. I start to pick up the stuff off the bed. My notebook, writing planner, pens, snacks, and laptop are strewn about. I don't want to wreck anything, and it's clear I'm not getting anything else done tonight.

"I was thinking about you tonight." Kim walks over to me.
"Oh, yeah?"
"Mmm, it was dirty thoughts," she whispers, like she's embarrassed.
"Now that I like to hear." I smile.

Kim grabs me by the hips, and she's about to kiss me, but instead I duck and spin around her.

"Hey!" She frowns and spins to face me.

But the second she does, she turns green and covers her mouth. In a split second, she runs to the bathroom and vomits in the toilet. I follow behind her and kneel on the floor next to her. She throws up again, and I use one hand to flush it down while the other gathers her hair. I reach for a hair tie on the sink and spin her hair into a tight braid. It'll keep it out of her face and out of the splash zone. I rub her back gently as she continues getting sick.

I think about what snacks I have here and what might help. I'm thinking crackers, but then I remember she has celiac disease. Okay, what gluten-free snacks do I have here? I think my protein bars are gluten-free, and I have some gluten-free pretzels, too. I bought them as a surprise for the next time she came over in case she wanted a snack. Those shits cost seven dollars a bag, too! Like they're removing the gluten, why do they cost so much more than normal pretzels?!

That isn't important right now. At least I know I have something she can eat. I have seltzer, too. Maybe the bubbles will soothe her stomach.

"I'm sorry." She rests her cheek across her arm that leans on the side of the toilet.

"It's okay." I continue rubbing her back gently. "Do you still feel sick?"

Instead of answering, she throws up again. I flush once more. Thankfully I'm not someone who is grossed out by vomit or I'd be joining her. I guess that's one of the good things about growing up with so many siblings. When one of us got sick, we all got sick.

"I think I'm okay now." Kim looks at me with a pale face.

"Okay, I'll stand first and then help you up. Okay?"

Kim nods. "Can I wash my mouth out?"

"Sure, hold on." I stand and give her a little cup of mouth wash. She spits it into the toilet, and then I help her stand. She's wobbly on her feet, and I'm a little afraid she's going to pass out on me, so I wrap one arm under hers.

I bring her to the bed, and she sits down. I bend toward the floor and help her out of her sneakers and socks. Then I look at her. I don't want to embarrass her, but she has vomit on her shirt, and I don't want her sleeping like that.

"I'm going to give you a shirt, too, so I need to take this one off." I point to the shirt she's wearing.

"Okay." She nods but she's like a bobblehead.

I help her out of the shirt, glad she's not getting the wrong idea about this. I know she came here with an idea of what might happen, but the second I saw how drunk she was, I knew that wasn't happening. I'm glad she had a fun night out with her friends, but I am a little pissed that they didn't make sure she got home okay. That friend's fiancé is a piece of work. Who the fuck left a drunk woman at someone else's doorstep?

I slide Kim into one of my oversized shirts and then pull back the covers. "Do you have a phone somewhere?"

"Yes!" Kim proudly grabs it from her front pocket.

I click it on and it's blowing up with tons of texts. I can't read any of them because it's locked. I'm about to ask her to use her Face ID when I see an incoming call from a contact named Ryleigh, who I remember as one of the friends she told me about. I click *accept* and say hello.

"Hello? Who the heck is this!?" She sounds pissed to hear someone else has Kim's phone.

"Ryleigh? This—"

"Look, you may not think it, but I can kick some serious ass, and I'm on my way over if you don't tell me where my best friend is!"

"Kim's here, drunk as hell and sleeping it off—"

"Wait, who is this?"

"This is Zara…I don't know if she—"

"Zara, the friend with benefits?"

"I see she's mentioned me. Yes."

"Oh, wait, how the hell did she get there?"

"She tells me your friend's fiancé dropped her off? Not too thrilled about that, by the way."

"I can come get her."

"No. I'm fine if she stays here. She got sick, and now she's sleeping it off. But I'm not thrilled your friend's fiancé just left her here when she was that wasted." I frown.

"Yeah… I agree. I'm sorry for yelling at you."

"It's alright." I smile.

"I thought you were kidnapping my best friend. I could see she wasn't home, but her location looked like it was on the beach, and I knew she had a lot to drink. I got worried."

"I understand. Look, my full name is Zara Grey, I'm in room 412 at the Harbor Inn. The moment Kim wakes up, I'll have her call or text you."

"Okay, she's really asleep?"

"I can send a picture if you'd like. She's passed out in my bed. And honestly, I'm a little worried about how much alcohol she consumed, so I'll be up for a bit making sure she doesn't choke on vomit."

"You sure you don't want me to come get her?"

"I assume you were drinking too, so she's probably safer here."

"That's true. Okay, thank you Zara."

We say goodbye, and I put Kim's phone on *do not disturb* and connect it to the charger. Kim is fast asleep on my pillow, so I grab my writing stuff and make a spot on the other side of the bed. I open a second Diet Coke, and I'm grateful for the caffeine. I put a bottle of water and some Motrin on her nightstand. She'll probably have a killer headache in the morning, and she'll be super dehydrated.

I slip into bed next to her and open my laptop. Suddenly, all the things I was questioning before become clear. I know exactly what I want this scene to be and how to write it. I make notes in my notebook before drafting it on my computer. I'm typing away for hours, snacking and sipping my drink. Kim sleeps quietly next to me. I check on her a few times when she's silent for too long. She's breathing, so I let her sleep. I don't have anything to do tomorrow, so I'll catch up on my sleep then.

At some point, I finish the few chapters I'm working on, and I see the sun starting to rise. Kim has been peacefully sleeping for hours at this point and seems fine. A quick Google search tells me she's probably okay since she hasn't gotten sick again. I turn out the lights and decide to get a little bit of sleep. I don't think I've ever taken care of someone like this—aside from family—but if this is what it's like to be in a relationship, I don't think I mind it…

At least not when it comes to Kim.

FOURTEEN

Kim

My phone rings, and I reach for it without opening my eyes. Oh, shit. Why does my head hurt so bad? Did I really have that much to drink last night? I pull the phone to my ear and wince.

"Kim? Can you open the door?" Ryleigh says on the other end of the phone.

"Ryleigh?" I am so disoriented.

"Yeah, I have breakfast. I thought you could use it."

"Can you use your key? I really don't want to get out of bed." I have given all the girls a key for emergencies, and this feels like the perfect opportunity to try it out.

"Uh, I'm not at your apartment. Are you at your apartment? Last I checked, you still weren't…"

My eyes shoot open, and I sit up in a panic as I drop my phone. I'm not at my apartment?! Where the hell am I? I drop the phone as I take in the familiar surroundings. Oh, thank god. I'm in Zara's room at the Inn. Zara is sleeping soundly next to me. Wait—how the hell did I get here? I try to think back to last night, but everything is a blur, and my head hurts the more I try to recall. I hear Ryleigh's voice calling my name and remember dropping my phone. Quickly, I pick it up and hold it to my ear again.

"I'm here."

"So are you letting me in or not?"

"You… you're at the Inn? How did—"

"I'm holding coffee and bagels and running out of arm strength. Can you just open the door?" she says impatiently.

"Okay, hold on."

I put down the phone and look down at my body. Am I wearing Zara's shirt? Where did my clothes go? We didn't have sex last night, did we? My pulse starts to race until I realize my panties are still very much on. I shake Zara awake, hoping she can fill in the many blanks I have.

"Hmm?" Zara mumbles.

"Hey, I'm sorry to bother you, but I'm very hungover and confused, and I think my best friend is here?" It sounds fake even as I say it aloud.

"Ryleigh?" she yawns.

"Yes…"

"I'm dressed, you can let her in." She stretches, and I nod.

"It's about time. I almost dropped this stuff out here." Ryleigh pushes her way in and plops the iced coffee tray and bag of food on the desk.

"Uh, can someone tell me what's going on?" I look around the room, confused.

"You went out with the gang last night. We all did a lot of shots at Teddy's and called it a night," Ryleigh says.

"You showed up drunk as a skunk on my doorstep," Zara adds, smiling as she gets out of bed. "I'm Zara, by the way. Nice to put a face to the name."

"I'm Ryleigh. Sorry again about the yelling. I brought apology coffee." She hands Zara a large coffee, and Zara smiles.

"You yelled at her?" I look at my best friend with wide eyes.

"Oh yes, she thought I was kidnapping you." Zara laughs.

"Ryleigh!"

Inn Love

"Well, in my defense, you didn't text me that you got home safe. So I checked your location, and it looked like you were on the beach, and then she picked up the phone. I thought she was holding you hostage or something." Ryleigh shrugs.

"So I explained who I was, gave her all my info, and told her you'd be staying here since you fell asleep in my bed."

Now it's my turn to blush. How freaking embarrassing am I?

"I'm so sorry," I mumble.

"It's all good." Zara waves me off, but I don't feel any better.

"I thought you'd be hungover, so I brought gluten-free pastries from that store in town and coffee from Love in a Cup," Ryleigh explains.

"How did I even get here?"

"Uh, you told me your friend's fiancé dropped you off," Zara says awkwardly.

"Will? Where the hell was Alana?"

"Supposedly, she was asleep. I called her this morning, and she had no idea, but yeah, Will said he thought you were fine," Ryleigh adds.

"Will dropped me off at the motel without checking that I actually knew someone staying here and just drove home?!" I am shocked. Will is sort of a stranger to the group, but I never thought he'd do something like that.

"Alana and Will got into it when I was on the phone with them. She's really sorry, and she said she'll call later. But they were like, screaming at each other about it." Ryleigh winces.

"Shit."

"Hey, that's not your fault. He did a shitty thing, and she should be mad at him. It's one thing if he dropped you at home or directly to me, but he let you wander around here drunk off your ass." Zara looks pissed, like someone sat on her cat or let her dog run free.

"Can I use your bathroom?" Ryleigh asks, changing the subject.

Zara nods, motioning to it, and I sit down, trying to piece

together last night. I don't usually drink so much that I black out. That's scary.

"I didn't want to say it in front of Ryleigh, but you sort of threw up last night. Like, a lot. And on your clothes. That's why you have that shirt on," Zara whispers next to me.

"Oh, my goodness." I put my face in my hands.

"Hey, it's okay. We all let loose sometimes. I'm just glad you're okay. I was a bit worried seeing you so sick." Zara takes my hands in hers.

"I'm so sorry. I never drink like that. I don't think I've ever even blacked out before. That's so scary. I'm glad I ended up here and you took care of me."

"We didn't have sex or anything, by the way. I'm sure it's scary if you can't remember, but you sort of tried to kiss me. I ducked, and then you threw up. I only took off your shirt so you would be clean," Zara explains.

"Thank you for taking care of me. I didn't think... if I was that drunk, I know you wouldn't take advantage of me. But thank you for the reassurance. I'm sorry I got sick. I'm sorry I tried to kiss you. I'm really sorry."

"Look, I only ducked because of how much you drank. If you were sober, it wouldn't have been an issue. This doesn't change anything. I sat next to you writing and only fell asleep like two hours ago."

"Really?"

"Yeah. I was worried you'd choke on your vomit or something."

"I really appreciate you taking care of me."

"Thank you for that. Are you ready to go, Kim? I thought I'd give you a ride home." Ryleigh smiles coming out of the bathroom.

"Yeah, let me grab my..." I look around the room for my shirt, and Zara hands me a plastic bag.

"I'm gonna get back to sleep, but I'll text you later to make plans this week. Okay?" Zara smiles.

"Okay. That sounds good." I relax a little, all my emotions still heightened from the night before.

That's something I've always hated about drinking. It's like your emotions go into overdrive the next day as your body struggles to get back to normal.

I follow Ryleigh to her car, and the second we're inside, I let the tears fall. I feel like such an idiot. Ryleigh's quiet as she drives. The radio on low is the only sound as we're directed to my apartment. When we pull up to my place, Ryleigh finally speaks.

"Are you okay?"

"I just feel like such an idiot. Why didn't I just go home? Why didn't Will just drop me home? And why did she take care of me? She probably thinks I'm some clingy, drunken fool now."

"You know I always give it to you straight. I don't know about Will. That was just an asshat move, but Alana's taking care of him. I think you went there because you like her, and that's where you feel safe. And as for why she took care of you, frankly, I think she's falling for you just as much as you are for her."

"What?" I wipe my eyes and look at her.

"I saw the way she was looking at you today. And I talked to her last night. Anyone else in her position would've happily dumped your drunken ass on my lap. But she thought about what was best for you. Heck, she even told me not to come over since she knew I had been out with you. She didn't seem angry or anything, and I even yelled at her!"

"Really?"

"Yes! She gave me all her information and even promised to make sure you would call and text me in the morning. I have a feeling she stayed up for a while to make sure you didn't die. She was really worried about you."

"Yeah, she said she stayed up to make sure I didn't choke."

"Exactly. That's not something you do for someone you don't care about. I know you both said it would just be friends with benefits, but I also think you're both lying to yourselves by saying it isn't something more."

I don't know what to say, so I don't say anything.

"Do you want me to come in?" Ryleigh offers.

"No, I think I need to be alone for a bit."

"Okay, call me if you need me." Ryleigh smiles.

I head inside with my bag of puke clothes and my too big T-shirt that smells like Zara, and then I kick off my shoes. I decide a shower is what I need first. I toss the T-shirt on the bed, having a feeling I'll want it after the shower. As I stand in the bathroom, I look at my hair and realize it's in a braid. But it's some sort of fancy braid I definitely don't know how to do—even sober. Did Zara braid my hair? Probably so I wouldn't get vomit in it. That small sentiment means more than I can explain.

I slowly unbraid my hair and step into the steaming shower. I scrub myself clean and brush my teeth twice. I put the T-shirt back on along with a fresh pair of panties. Then, I look for some Tylenol and a big glass of water. I'm going to sleep this hangover off, but first I need to replenish my body. I check that I locked the front door and head to my bed.

Before I close my eyes, I check my phone to make sure it's charged. There I find a text from Zara.

Zara: Baseball game on Tuesday? Have a feeling you'd look cute in a baseball cap! 😊

I hold my phone to my chest with a rush of emotions. I was worried Zara wouldn't want to see me again after that disaster of a night. I mean I got drunk, tried to kiss her, got rejected, and threw up in front of her. What sane person would still want to see me after? Instead of ghosting me, she's making plans and flirting with me when she should be sleeping.

My feelings for her are definitely real, and that scares the crap out of me. I could overthink it and stress like I usually do. But instead, I lock my phone and shut my eyes. I'll text her back when I wake up.

Maybe I'm falling for her, and maybe she's falling for me, too. And maybe this time, instead of stressing about it, I'll just see what happens. I could spend the rest of the time I have with her this summer getting to know her. We can just see what happens when the summer ends. And maybe it won't be so bad if she breaks my heart.

Because at least I'll have the chance to fall in love with her.

FIFTEEN

Zara

"You should know, I know nothing about baseball," Kim tells me.

"Well, you couldn't tell by your outfit." I laugh. She is dressed in a baseball jersey for a team I've never heard of, with a crop top underneath and a pair of black short shorts.

"I borrowed this from Norah. She said it's from a fictional baseball team." Kim smiles.

"That makes more sense. I just thought it would be something fun to do. I can't remember the last time I went to a game. Plus, it's out of town, so if it's okay with you, we can have some PDA." I wink.

Kim blushes just like I hoped she would and nods.

"You have to protect me from any fly balls, though. I don't want a black eye."

"I don't think that's possible. There's usually a net or something up."

"Well, my face seems to be a magnet for balls, so who knows."

I try to hold it in, but I burst out laughing. Full belly laughter I can't contain.

"What are you... Oh my god! You can't be serious! I didn't mean it like that!" Kim scolds me.

"You're the one who said it!" I laugh.

"Yeah, yeah, get your laughs in." She rolls her eyes.

"I'm sorry, I apparently have the mind of a teenage boy."

"Yes, you do." Kim pretends she's still mad, but I can tell from the smile she's holding back that she's not.

"Don't worry, I'll keep your pretty face protected."

"Moving on! Where are we supposed to park?"

I pull up the information on my phone and read it aloud.

"It says in the East parking lot. I think it's that one." I point.

Kim pulls in, we scan our tickets and parking pass and look for a spot. I slide out of the car and take Kim's hand as we walk in. The whole point of going somewhere out of town was so we could have a little PDA. It would be rare for one of her students to see her here in a stadium this big. I like the way her fingers wrap around mine.

"Snacks?" I point to the concession stand.

"Hmm, maybe popcorn?" she asks, thinking out loud.

I lead her to the line, and when it's our turn, I speak first. "Is the popcorn gluten-free? And safe from cross-contamination?"

"Yes, we only use butter on it, and the scoop stays inside it for popcorn only," the worker informs us.

"Perfect, we'll have one large and two Diet Cokes, please."

I take out my wallet, and Kim tries to stop me. "I'm paying, put your wallet away."

"Are you sure?"

"Shush, I got this." I hand the worker a twenty and put a five-dollar bill in the tip jar.

"Thanks," Kim mumbles. I can tell no one has ever tried to take care of her like this before. And I'm doing the bare minimum here.

"Let's find our seats."

I hold the popcorn, and Kim holds the drinks. I'd try to hold everything, but I know it would end up on the ground.

Our seats are right behind third base. I figured it would be a good spot to see the game. Thankfully, a lot of the seats in this section are empty, so we don't have to worry about being cramped. We make ourselves comfortable, sit down with our snacks, and start digging into the popcorn. Kim has this big smile on her face as the game starts, and I realize I've made the right choice in bringing her here.

"How did you get these seats? We're, like, super close."

"Don't worry, I'm still protecting that face from any foul balls." I wink. "My sister's husband is on the team. He plays second base." I point him out and wave.

"Holy crap, that's sort of cool."

"Eh, he's one of my favorite brothers-in-law. But he travels a lot with my sister and the kids, so he loses some points for that." I shrug.

"Are your sisters here?"

"No, I asked, but they're all busy. Most of them have kids, so they have a calendar of events to follow them to."

"Thank you for checking on the popcorn. I know it's simple, but it's appreciated. Not everyone remembers."

"No worries, you told me once, so I committed it to memory." I squeeze her leg lightly, and she smiles.

I hate how effortless it is to be with her. It's like everything about us just makes sense. Except for the fact that I live in New York and she lives in Lovers. I feel like I can be myself with her, and I feel safe with her. I don't mind spending all my time with her—in fact, I welcome it. I've never been one to want to spend all my free time with someone, but here I am. I could be doing a million other things right now, but I'm more than content just being here with her.

"So, I assume we're rooting for your brother-in-law's team?" She points at the field.

"Yup, they're the Blue Hawks. Hence my very cute and very free merch." I show off the T-shirt I'm wearing. I usually wear it as a nightshirt, so it was something I had packed with me.

Kim tosses a piece of popcorn in her mouth, and I watch her lips—puckered, pink, and begging to be kissed. I wait until she swallows the popcorn, then I lean in for a kiss. Grabbing her face and pulling her toward me, I'm feverish with desire. I want to feel her on me. I slip my tongue into her mouth, and she groans. I taste the buttery, salty flavor of her tongue. Fuck, she tastes even better than normal. Her hand grazes my cheek before sliding into my hair. Before it gets too heated for public, I pull back, and Kim is blushing ear to ear.

"Wow," she mutters quietly.

I take a sip of my Diet Coke and smile. My eyes float back to the game, watching the players run around the field. The other team is up, their batter at two strikes. I assume it's going to be a third until, at the last second, he hits it. The ball comes flying our way, and my eyes widen as I realize it might actually be coming right toward us. I drop my soda into the cup holder and lean over Kim to protect her. This is what she was afraid of happening, and I'll be damned if I don't hold up my promise. I shield her with my body and close my eyes—until I hear the crowd cheer behind us. I peek open one eye and realize a family six rows above us caught the ball. I guess my depth perception was a little off, but at least she's okay.

"Sorry, I didn't know if it would... it looked like it was coming toward us." I grimace.

"You actually saved me, just like you said you would." Kim looks surprised.

"Yeah, I didn't want it to hit you."

"But you legit just went into protective mode and shielded me with your body." Kim stares at me in awe.

"Yeah." I shrug. It was no big deal—I just didn't want her to get hurt.

Kim surprises me by grabbing me by the shirt and kissing me fiercely. She definitely doesn't care who's watching, because I can hear people around us hollering and cheering, but she doesn't stop. If anything, that encourages her. Her tongue slips into my mouth, and this time, I'm the one groaning. Holy fuck. I wrap my arms around her, and we're both almost falling out of our seats to get closer. Eventually, we both need air, so she pulls away and smiles at me with a devilish look. My lipstick is all over her mouth, so I'm sure mine is messed up too. But Kim just reaches for my hand and tosses a piece of popcorn in her mouth like nothing happened, which leaves me more stunned than I care to admit.

She glances at me sideways and winks, and I swear it takes everything not to pull her into the stadium bathroom and fuck her right there. How the hell is she this hot? It has to be freaking illegal.

"You got a little drool." She touches the side of her mouth, teasing me.

"My lipstick is all over your face." I laugh.

"Eh." She shrugs and leaves it there like it's no big deal.

SIXTEEN

Kim

Zara moans from the passenger seat, and my grip on the steering wheel gets tighter. I swear if we didn't already have a run in with the state trooper, I would pull over and eat her out right here. Zara has her fingers down her shorts, and I wish they were mine. I can hear how wet she is and how badly she's dying to be touched. I'm pushing every speed limit by nine miles, the exact amount just before they can ticket you. I'm switching lanes and doing whatever I can to beat the GPS time of getting us home in eighteen minutes. That's way too fucking long. I've already shaved off seven minutes, and I'm determined to keep going.

"Mmm," Zara hums and I glance down, noticing her fingers moving in a circular motion.

"You're killing me here." I groan.

"It's not my fault I can't touch you. You're driving."

"I know," I whine. I'm actually fucking whining over not being able to touch her or be touched. This is what we've resorted to.

"Think I can come before we get there?"

"Are you kidding me? You're going to make us crash."

"Got it, so I'll just keep teasing myself then." Zara laughs to herself.

We hit a red light, and I actually curse.

"Someone's really pent up, huh?"

"I wasn't until you kept kissing me today." I wiggle in my seat. My panties are ruined, and Zara is to blame.

Zara dips her fingers lower, and I can literally hear how wet she is. Fuck. This is torture. She shouldn't be allowed to be this hot. The light turns green, and I speed through. There's a shortcut to my road, and I'm going to take it.

"I can't wait to feel your lips on me instead of my fingers." Zara pulls her fingers out of her panties and turns them toward me. "Want a taste?"

She's teasing me, but I'm so horny I don't even care. I keep my eyes on the road but open my mouth. Zara slips her fingers in, and I suck them dry. God, she tastes so fucking sweet. She's like a dessert I'll never get enough of. I let go of her fingers, and she giggles.

"We're going to be there in two minutes, and I want you naked the second we get inside," I tell her.

"Yes ma'am." She salutes me, and although it's a joke, I think it's sort of hot.

I pull into my assigned spot and dig my key out of my purse. Zara's quickly behind me, realizing I wasn't joking about getting inside. As I'm unlocking the door, Zara's kissing my neck, and I no longer care if someone can see because it feels to freaking good. The door closes behind us, and I push her body up against it. Zara's slipping the T-shirt off over her head while I drop to my knees. I take off her shorts and press my face to her pussy.

"Oh, fuck!" Zara screams the moment my tongue touches her.

I suck on her clit, harder than I normally would, but she doesn't complain. In fact, she gets even wetter. She's whimpering, pulling my hair tightly with her fingers. She tries playing with her breasts, and I push her hand to the side, pulling and tugging on her nipples until they're hard and taut. I bite the insides of her thighs and place kisses along there, too. She's moaning, probably close enough to come and I stop, standing up and start walking to my bedroom.

Zara doesn't follow me, but I can hear her baffled breathing.

"What the hell was that?" Zara walks in naked and confused.

"Payback for teasing me in the car." I smirk. I had tossed off my clothes and am sitting on the edge of the bed.

"You devil." She shakes her head at me. But I know she's just impressed because she didn't see it coming.

"I'm not letting you come until you make me come." I cross my arms over my chest.

"Deal." Zara pushes my shoulders, so I fall back into the bed as she crawls on top of me.

Her hands are on my chest; my nipples are hard and sensitive. She kisses me, stopping to lick my neck to my collar bone and then back to kissing. She was building me up, but we both knew I didn't need it. I reach down to touch myself and she pushes my hand away. Zara ties back her hair with a hair tie and then flips around so her pussy is in my face and mine is in hers. Knowing I can't resist the taste of her, I pull her thighs toward me and lick.

At the same time, she flattens her tongue, swiping it across my clit, and I cry out her name against her. It's all muffled between her thighs. My grip on her gets tighter as she edges me. Her sweet wetness drips down my chin, and I'm unable to lick her fast enough. I've never seen anyone get so turned on while eating someone else out. I take my time licking her swollen slit, knowing how badly she wants me to make her come. I also know, with just a few swipes of my tongue across her clit, she'll squirt all over me. But I'm determined to keep her waiting. I want to come first, and she's getting payback for teasing me in the car.

Her body bucks above me as I stick my tongue inside her. She retaliates by sucking harder on my clit, causing me to cry out her name. Then, she dips in two fingers, swirling them around inside me before folding them to hit my G-spot. I let go of her thighs, unable to keep eating her out while she does this. I'm so fucking close and I want to come so bad. Zara hums against my clit, sucking it while pumping her fingers in and out of me. My head falls back as far as it can go, and my back raises off the bed.

"Yes! Yes! Oh, yes!" I cry out.

I expect Zara to stop, but she keeps going, somehow getting a second orgasm out of me. The second one crashing even harder than the first. I'm breathless as she lets go and slaps my sensitive pussy for good measure.

"My turn." Zara climbs back so her pussy is on my face. She lowers herself.

Without catching my breath or opening my eyes, I play with Zara. Sucking on her clit, biting just the tiniest bit and causing her to yelp out, and moving my tongue as fast as I can to make her finish. She rides my face like a roller coaster, gripping the headboard. She's so close. I feel her tightening, and then she screams my name.

"Kim! Oh, yes baby! Yes!" She keeps riding my face, her juices squirting everywhere, and I lap it all up.

Zara falls to the side, and we both try to catch our breath. Neither of us speak for what feels like a long time. Eventually, Zara reaches for my hand and squeezes it gently. She gets off the bed, and I assume she's going to the bathroom. She isn't gone for long before returning.

"I'm going to wipe your face, but it's a clean washcloth," she whispers quietly.

I'm too tired to say anything so I just nod. The washcloth is warm, almost hot, as she drags it delicately across my face. Then she brings it to my pussy, and I whimper, still sensitive. She wipes my folds and my inner thighs before leaving again. When she returns, I open an eye, and she smiles at me. Her lipstick is smudged, almost gone at this point, and her hair is a fluffy mess and falling out of her ponytail. But fuck, she looks gorgeous. It's like I can see past all of that and just see her. This amazing person.

Zara pulls the covers over us, and I move closer to her. We're face-to-face, both of us lying on our sides on the pillows. Neither of us say anything, but it's like we're saying a lot. Her fingers find mine, and we hold hands. Our breathing has normalized, so it's quiet—except for the sounds outside. I hear a few birds and someone mowing a lawn nearby.

Sleep wants to take over, but I don't want to miss this moment. I want to soak it all in, commit it to memory. Zara has a little scar on her cheek, and I wonder how she got it. It looks like, at one point, she had a nose ring—a tiny hole that never quite healed right. I feel like there are a million things I don't know about her, and I want to know everything. I mean, people never truly know someone completely. But I wish I knew her. I wish I had more than the summer to know her. I wish I had more time. I can tell I'm going to cry, and there's no way to stop it. So I quickly get up, sit on the edge of the bed, and let Zara know I'm going to shower.

"Do you want company?" she asks quietly. I think she can tell something's wrong, but she's not sure if she should say anything.

"I don't think my shower is quite big enough." I force a laugh and head to the bathroom.

The second I'm in there, I turn on the water and quietly sob. It's not supposed to be like this. What the hell was the point of me meeting someone like Zara if it'll just be another ending and I'll have to say goodbye? Is there a lesson to learn here? It all feels like a mean joke from the universe. Zara and I feel like nothing I've ever had before, and it's going to be over before it even fully starts. How can that be our story?

I get in the shower and get clean, realizing I can't just leave the bathroom still dirty. The shower helps a bit, and it at least washes the tears away. When I get out, my bed is empty, and my heart sinks a little. I guess it's for the best. I know what this is, why would I expect her to stick around? I get dressed and throw my hair in a bun without brushing it. Then, I head to the kitchen. Maybe I have some ice cream in the freezer or something.

"Hey, I didn't hear you get out." Zara's standing, mostly naked, in my kitchen. She's just wearing the T-shirt of hers she let me borrow last week.

"What are you doing?" I look around confused.

"I was going to make us something to eat, but you don't have much. I settled for eggs and toast. Is that okay? I'm starving, so I figured you are too." She smiles.

"Yeah." I nod. "I-I, uh, thought you left."

"No, I mean I can go if you wanna be alone." She slides a plate in front of me at the sad excuse of a kitchen table I have. Then she grabs her plate, setting it across from me.

"Thank you." I smile, picking up my fork.

"It's all gluten-free, I mean, not that you have gluten in the house, I assume."

"I don't. But good to know." I take a bite of eggs and groan. Damn, I'm hungrier than I thought.

"You okay? Your shower good?" The way she asks tells me she knows something's up. But I appreciate her subtle way of asking.

"My shower was good," I assure her.

Maybe this is all we have, but at least I won't forget it.

SEVENTEEN

Zara

"I didn't know you had a backyard," I say, following Kim outside the door from the kitchen.

"It's small, but it has two trees, so I put up a hammock." She shrugs.

"Um, can we please go test out the hammock?" I probably look like a dog chasing a ball. But a little-known fact about me is that I love hammocks.

"Of course." She laughs and holds it steady for me to climb in.

"We had one growing up, I used to spend hours reading in it every day."

"That sounds relaxing." Kim settles in next to me, I can smell her shampoo under my head.

"It was. I think it was the only quiet place in my house. My sisters didn't like it and would rather run around the yard or do sports. It was kind of a safe haven for me," I admit.

"I like it out here because I can think. It's always quiet, and the sun doesn't shine in your face because of the trees. It's relaxing," she adds.

"This feels like the perfect place to smoke pot, honestly."

Kim looks at me and raises an eyebrow. "Do you have some?"

"I, uh, have my weed pen in my bag in the car," I admit. "Do you smoke pot?"

"I used to in college. I haven't in years, but I wouldn't say no." She smiles.

"Do you want me to get it?"

"Only if you want to."

"I'll be right back." I place a kiss on her lips and head to the car. I grab her keys on the way out, and I'm back outside in five minutes.

"Kids have it so easy these days. You can just buy a little discreet device. When I was a kid, you had to know someone to buy weed and then learn how to roll a joint," Kim says, looking at the pen.

"You just sounded about three hundred years old." I laugh.

"Is it strong?"

"Not really. It might be if you're not used to it. I don't do it all the time, but often when I'm writing."

I hand the pen to Kim, and she takes a small breath in, then blows out some smoke. She does it a few more times, finally getting the hang of it, and on the last one, she coughs when she takes in too much smoke. She hands it back to me, and I take a longer hit, taking my time before letting it go. Kim watches me as I do, still lying in the hammock.

"You do it so gracefully," she muses.

I hand the pen back to her and climb into the hammock again. Kim takes a few more hits, this time not as hard, and she seems to relax. I have always been a fan of weed—it's one of the safer drugs in my mind. I feel relaxed and at ease with it, and it isn't as addicting as some people claim. I play with my hair, twirling the ends between my fingers. I'd love to play with Kim's, but hers is wet from the shower, and I don't want to undo her bun.

"Damn, I forgot how fun this is."

"They drug test you at school?" I guess.

"Yeah. It's random, so I wouldn't be able to do this during the school year. I just had one when I got hired, or else I wouldn't take this risk."

"I think I want to make out with you." I run my finger down the side of her cheek.

"Hell yeah." Kim giggles.

I lean in to kiss her, and it feels euphoric. Kissing her normally feels amazing, but this is different. Our tongues move in unison, and it feels like I'm scratching an itch only she knows about. Her hands are like velvet over my skin. I lean into her touch, and she kisses me harder. Kim's leg hooks under mine, our feet playing footsie with each other. We are tangled in each other as much as we can be. It feels safe and easy with her. Kim pulls away, giggling, and although I have no idea why she's laughing, I start laughing too. Soon, all you can hear is the sound of the two of us hysterically laughing over nothing.

I stare up at the trees and wonder if we could climb them. They look sturdy enough to hold us—I mean, they can hold this hammock well enough. I was never good at climbing trees; I have the upper body strength of a penguin. So maybe climbing trees is out of the question. Maybe I could carve our initials into the tree. It couldn't be that hard to do, right? People are always doing that in rom-coms. It's sort of romantic and fun. But I don't carry any kind of knife with me. Maybe a kitchen knife would work? Surely, I'd have to ask Kim before I disappear into her kitchen and return with a knife. I don't want her to scream, thinking I'm attempting to murder her or something.

"I want to carve something in the tree," I tell Kim.

"Okay, how do we do that?"

"Do you have any knives?"

"Uh, in my kitchen. But I don't know how sharp they are."

"I'll be back."

I hop out of the hammock and head inside to investigate the knife situation. She has a handful of butter knives and even a few steak knives, but I need something a little sturdier. I notice the block of knives on the counter and take the smallest one. It looks like it could do the job. I walk back outside, and Kim's eyes are closed like she's sleeping.

"I found one," I say quietly and hold up the knife.

Kim wastes no time, kicking me in the crotch and flipping out of the hammock.

Except she gets stuck in the hammock like a cocoon and starts spinning back and forth. My knife falls blade-first into the grass, and I groan, grabbing my crotch. How could it hurt so bad when I don't really have anything there? Kim is hysterically laughing in the hammock as I spin it to get her out.

"I'm so sorry! Are you okay?"

"I am now. Why the hell did you do that?" I groan.

"I forgot what you went to do. I think I dozed off for a few minutes, and then I saw you with the knife, I got panicked, and I went into self-defense mode."

"Well, you definitely don't need to take any more classes. You've got the crotch-kicking down to a science."

"I guess that's good to know."

"I was going to carve the tree." I point and pick up the knife.

I sit down on the grass next to the tree and drag the knife through the trunk. Except nothing really happens—all you can see is a small scratch. I do it again, this time with a little more force, but the same thing happens.

"What are you doing?" Kim sits down next to me.

"I was trying to carve something into the tree, but apparently, that's a lot harder than I thought it would be." I frown.

"It looks simple in the movies."

"That's what I was thinking!"

I try a few more times and only manage the first line of the letter K. There's no way this is going to work with this kind of knife. I adjust my grip and hold it a little differently, hoping this will work, but as soon as I try, the knife snaps in half. I mean, legit—the handle is in my hand, and the blade part is stuck in the tree. Kim and I look at each other in shock and then start cracking up. Not even because of the weed—just because it's that fucking funny.

"Let's bring this inside and get some snacks," Kim suggests.

I pull the knife blade out of the tree and follow her inside. She tells me to toss the knife in the garbage and starts looking in the cabinets for some snacks. We just ate, so I'm not super hungry, but I can tell she's got a case of the munchies. She pulls down a bag of Cheetos and gluten-free Oreos.

"You know, I was thinking... how come I've never read one of your books?" she says between bites. Her mouth is full of food, but somehow, she still looks adorable. She's sitting on the counter, holding the bag of Cheetos in one hand and the Oreos open next to her.

"I don't know." I shrug.

"Can I read them?"

"I mean, yeah, they're available for anyone." I laugh.

"I know, but is that okay? I know some artists prefer their... the people around them not to read their work."

"Oh, nah, I'm okay with it. It's really dark, though, so please check the trigger warnings first. I don't want you getting upset or, like, scarred for life."

"That's fair." Kim nods.

EIGHTEEN

Kim

"Holy shit, if that's what you're wearing, then I definitely want to come," Zara says over FaceTime. I'm spinning in my dress for the bachelorette party. I ordered it online and it only got here yesterday, which is why I'm mentally freaking out about how short it is.

"I'd love for you to come, but it's Alana's special night and I have to be there to hold back her hair."

"I know, but damn. You always look good, but wow."

"It's not too short? I don't really have anything else because Alana insisted we all wear black."

"I mean, don't bend over in it, but I think you look great."

"Okay." I pick up my phone and move it to my dresser so I can do my makeup and talk.

Zara watches quietly as I apply mascara, eyeliner, and eyeshadow. Not in that order, obviously. Alana's fiancé Will is driving Alana and I to the party and then picking us up after. I'm going to stay with them tonight, so we don't have to make two trips home later. I already explained this to Zara, who made a face when I mentioned Will.

"Look, just call me if you get too drunk, okay? I can call you an Uber or, like, teleport there. I don't like that Will's the one bringing you home—considering last time." Zara frowns.

"I know. I'm not going to be drinking too much, trust me. I didn't enjoy not knowing where half of my night went." I sigh.

"Well, have fun, and text me if you need anything!" Zara says before we hang up. I promise to send her a sexy pic from the bar bathroom.

Alana texts me to let me know she's here, and I grab my overnight bag and phone before heading out the door. It's a little chilly outside, considering the sun already set. I'm showing way more leg than normal, but at least the party is indoors.

"Hi, babe!" Alana smiles from the driver's seat. Will sits next to her on his phone, offering me a simple hello without looking up.

"Are you ready for tonight?" I ask.

"Oh, yes! I'm so excited. And I love your dress! So sexy." Alana winks at me in the rearview mirror, and I blush.

"Thanks." I want to say how I feel about it, but with Will here, I feel more awkward than normal. I want to be supportive, but he's still a stranger among the group—and it isn't like we haven't tried to change that. But for some reason, he has no interest in getting to know the people in Alana's life.

So instead, it's awkwardly quiet as we make our way to the bar. Gemma rented out Teddy's for the night, and Alana doesn't know it yet, but we also hired a stripper. I can't wait to see the look on her face when the stripper comes out.

When we arrive, Alana steps out and fixes her dress. It's white A-line dress with lace long sleeves and white heels. She turns around to grab her purse, and I can see her veil is actually an oversized tulle bow flowing through her dark curls.

"You look so cute!" I gush. She looks like something off someone's Pinterest board.

"Can I have the keys? I can still catch the end of the game if I go now." Will sticks out his hand. Alana hands him the keys, and he leans in for a kiss, but she turns her cheek. He looks annoyed but doesn't say anything.

"Ready?" Alana smiles at me. I try to pretend everything about that was normal.

I follow her inside, and everyone cheers. It isn't a surprise really, but Alana loves the attention. I slip away to find our friends while she stops to say hello to everyone. Heather's taking photos with a woman I've never seen before while Wrenn and Ryleigh are hanging on each other. Norah's hanging out by the bar with Gemma—who's looking at her a little more than friendly. I wonder if something is going on there. I'll have to remind myself to sus that out later.

"How do you not have a drink yet?" Ryleigh reaches for a drink and hands it to me.

I smile and take a small sip. After last time, I'm taking it slow. I want to pace myself. Everyone always warns about the effects of alcohol, but no one talks about how scary it can be to black out. I don't want to go down that road again.

I'm introduced to Heather's girlfriend, Sage, and I realize I could've invited Zara tonight. Is it too late to call her now? I know she isn't up to much, but I don't want her to feel like an afterthought. Besides, I'm staying at Alana's tonight, and Zara probably has writing she needs to do.

There's music playing, so Ryleigh convinces me to dance, and I see a bunch of people we went to high school with. I didn't realize Alana had kept in touch with so many people. I make more small talk than I'd like, especially when most of it comes with the usual questions of *are you seeing anyone?* It seems like everyone our age is married or getting married, or at least seriously paired up. And for the first time in my life, I'm happy not to be. Whatever I have with Zara is enough for now. She makes me happy, and that's what counts.

I'm on drink number two when I have to pee, so I excuse myself to the bathroom. While in here, I realize I'm alone, so I slide down my dress to see the lingerie bodysuit I'm wearing under it and snap a picture to send to Zara. It's just enough to tease her. I don't think I've sent a half-naked selfie since high school, and I forgot how fun it can be. I double check I'm clicking Zara and not someone else, then I press *send*. A photo is worth a thousand words.

I quickly fix my dress and return to the party. My phone buzzes almost immediately.

Zara: You've got to be kidding me
    Zara: The dress was bad enough, but this?!
    Zara: How far away are you? Asking for a friend.
    Zara: Definitely using this to get myself off...

I blush. Zara has a way about her that makes me feel more sexy and wanted than I ever had before. I decide to text her back later and enjoy more of the party. I realize I haven't seen Alana in a while when Norah pulls me aside to tell me it's stripper time. I get a front row seat to drunk Alana throwing singles at our high school classmate. She's the most relaxed I've seen her all summer, despite an ass being in her face. Everyone is cheering her on, and when he's done with his performance, she convinces him to stay and join the party.

"I feel bad for whoever has to hold her hair back tonight." Ryleigh grimaces.

"Wouldn't that be Will?" Norah asks.

"Yeah, right." Wrenn scoffs.

"I'm sleeping over there tonight, so I guess it's me," I add.

"You're sleeping there? Good luck." Wrenn rolls her eyes. Before I can ask what that means, Ryleigh is ushering her away from everyone.

I know Wrenn and Alana weren't always the closest of sisters growing up, but I thought they were closer now. Maybe Wrenn had a problem with her future brother-in-law. It's different when your sister is getting married, I assume anyway. I'll have to ask Zara about that.

"I just love you guys so much," Alana slurs, tossing her arms over my and Gemma's shoulders. We steady her, realizing she's not wearing any shoes, and her bow is falling out of her hair.

"Time to call it a night?" Gemma looks at me, and I nod.

"No! I wanna stay and dance! I'm having so much fun!" Alana shakes her head, but she doesn't have much pull right now, considering how drunk she is.

"Maybe we should find her shoes first?" I suggest.

"You'll never guess where I hid them." Alana boops me on the nose and then burps.

"Okay, drunky, we should get you out of here," Gemma says.

"Where did you put your shoes?" I ask again.

"Did someone lose a pair of shoes?" Wrenn comes over, holding Alana's shoes in her hand.

"Aw, fuck." Alana frowns.

Gemma and I help her sit on the chair so we can get her shoes on. Wrenn bends down to put them on for her, and Alana giggles.

"That tickles!" She squirms.

"Please stop that." Wrenn is not in the mood.

"Oh, my grumpy little sis. I love you even if you're grumpy. I love you always!" Alana drunkenly kisses Wrenn's head.

"Do you need me to call Will?" Wrenn looks at us.

"Yes, please." I nod. I don't have his number, and it's not like Alana would comply with us right now.

Wrenn excuses herself to call while Alana complains about having to go home. The party is still going on, but with how wasted everyone is, I doubt they'd even notice the guest of honor was gone. Wrenn tells us Will is five minutes away, so we make our way to the front door, Alana hanging on Gemma and me, her feet sort of dragging behind us. At least we're tall—it wouldn't work if we were Wrenn and Ryleigh's heights.

"I didn't think she drank this much," Gemma comments.

"I did shots with everyone!" Alana elongates the word "everyone" and winks at us.

"We're waiting for Will, and we'll take care of you tonight," I tell her.

"He's so busy, I bet he won't," Alana mumbles.

I'm about to ask what she means when Will pulls up in front of us. The headlights blind us, but at least he sees us. We try to help Alana forward when she pukes on the front of Will's fancy car. I couldn't tell you what kind it is, but I know it's way out of my tax bracket. He jumps out of the car, and instead of checking on his fiancée, his eyes go wild with rage, looking at the car.

"Are you kidding me!?" he yells.

Everyone who is standing outside to smoke or wait for a ride looks over at us. Alana is standing up, but she's not in good shape. Will looks like he's about to explode when Gemma steps in.

"She's drunk off her ass. I'm sure she'll regret that tomorrow, but right now, you need to get her home," Gemma tells Will in a commanding tone. He looks like he wants to argue with her, but then he glances around at the crowd and nods.

Will takes Alana from us, and we help her into the back of the car. We figure it would be better for her to lie down, considering how wasted she is. I can tell Will is worried about the interior of his car, but there isn't much we can do. Gemma and I make sure she's okay before I get in the passenger seat next to Will. He's out of the parking lot and heading toward their house in minutes.

"How the hell did she get that drunk?" Will whisper-yells at me.

"She was having fun. She said she was doing a lot of shots," I say quietly.

"You've got to be kidding me." He scoffs.

When we get to their place, he carries her into the apartment, and I carry our stuff. I assume he's going to tell me where I can sleep or give me a blanket, but he doesn't do that. Instead, I hear

Alana getting sick in the bathroom, so I go check on her. She's on the bathroom floor alone, and Will is nowhere to be found.

"Hey, you okay?" I sit with Alana as she gets sick. I run a washcloth under cold water and brush it against her forehead.

"Do you want to go to bed? Or do you need to throw up more?"

"I—I can go to bed. But I want to change. Can you get me clothes?" Alana looks like a heap on the floor.

"Of course. Which door?"

"Second to the left." She points, and I follow her instructions.

Walking into the bedroom, I find Will on his phone, sitting on the edge of the bed.

"Uh, Alana wanted some pajamas?"

"They're in there." He points to the dresser.

I find a pair of shorts and a cotton T-shirt. She should be comfortable in this tonight. I'm about to go when I realize I have something to say.

"Are you just leaving her there?" I ask Will.

"What?" He looks shocked that I'm actually speaking to him.

"Your fiancée is drunk off her ass and puking her guts out. Are you seriously just leaving her there on the bathroom floor?" I'm pissed. Zara had taken care of me, and I'd known her for less than three months. This was the man Alana was supposed to be marrying. Why the hell wasn't he getting her pajamas and holding a washcloth on her head?

"She's got to puke it out. She'll be fine." He shrugs.

"You're kidding, right? It was bad enough that you dropped me off somewhere other than my house when I was just as drunk. Maybe I was super convincing. Maybe you just didn't care. But this is your fucking fiancée. Don't you give at least a little bit of a shit about her well-being?" I'm raising my voice because I'm that angry.

"I can't handle a hysterical woman and a drunk woman." He rolls his eyes.

"Alana deserves better than you." I slam the door behind me.

Part of me hopes he'll prove me wrong and follow me out. But, of course, he doesn't. I bring Alana to the guest room I find on my way back to the bathroom. I help her change her clothes and settle into bed next to her. She falls asleep immediately, and despite how tired I am, I want to make sure she's okay. So I call Zara, knowing she'll still be up, and I ask her to stay awake with me until I'm positive Alana is okay. Not once does Will come to check on us, and in the morning, he's gone.

NINETEEN

Zara

"You really wanted to come see my classroom?" Kim says, unconvinced, as she staples together another stack of papers.

"Well, I wanted to see you, and you're here, so why not?" I shrug. I'm sitting on the edge of a student's desk playing with one of the fidget toys she had.

"It's not much, but it was a lot worse when I started. I'm pretty much done with everything until I get my roster, then I need to laminate the name tags for the cubbies," she says, looking over her checklist.

"Gotcha. I like the subtle nods to Harry Styles."

"You caught that?" Her eyes light up.

"Yes, I don't know if children will. But as someone who was around for One Direction, I caught it."

"Oh, god, when you put it like that, I feel so old." She laughs.

"Is anyone else here today?" I ask.

"I don't think so. I didn't see any other cars in the parking lot, and a lot of teachers wait until the last few weeks before school starts."

"Hmm." I purse my lips.

Kim's busy finishing stacking together some papers, so she doesn't notice when I walk over to the classroom door and lock it. I glance out the one window she had open and shut the blinds when I see the still empty parking lot. Then I walk over to Kim's desk and spin her chair to face me.

"W-what?"

"Miss Stewart, I've been a bad girl, and I think I need some extra attention." I'd never done the teacher/student fantasy before but if there was ever a time to try, it's now.

"Zara!" Kim blushes a deep red.

"Miss Stewart, I'd love to do some extra credit to make it up to you." I get down on my knees and Kim gasps.

"We're going to get into trouble."

"You said no one's around, Miss Stewart. But I can stop if you want me to. I'll do anything to be the teacher's pet." I look up at her, waiting for confirmation that this is okay. It's a big risk, but I can tell by the way she's looking at me that she wants to say yes.

"We have to be quick. And quiet." Kim spreads her legs and out peaks a pair of black lace panties.

I groan and move my face closer. But she closes her legs and puts her fingers on my chin, tilting my head to look at her again.

"You're going to eat me out until I come. You can't stop, and you can't make a sound. Understand? Now get under my desk," she commands me with what I assume is her teacher voice. I'm soaked and waiting to follow her every command.

I slip under the desk, get somewhat comfortable, and then she moves her chair, positioning it so my face is in her pussy. I push her panties to the side and lick her wet center. Kim clenches her fists on the arms of the chair, but she doesn't speak. I love how into this she is and how she won't make a sound even if no one was in the building. I swirl my tongue through her folds and hum against her as I taste her sweet juices. Thank god for the sundress she is wearing. The cotton fabric falls over my head, and I'm as concealed as I can be.

"Yes, just like that. Make me feel good," she whispers.

Suddenly, I want more of her praise. It feels different when it's coming with this fantasy. I want to make her satisfied as much as I want an A. I press my thighs together, my clit feeling like fire, begging to be touched. I knew I could probably slip a finger or two in my shorts without her knowing, but I want to please her, and part of that means making her come before I even get a tease. I'm sure she'll take care of me after. Or I'll do it when I get back to the Inn. Either way, this moment is all about making her feel good.

"Do you think you could eat me out on my desk?" she asks.

"Fuck yes." She moves the chair so I can come out and she climbs on her desk. It's mostly empty except for a few things which she quickly clears away.

Kim hitches her dress around her waist and kicks her panties aside. I pick them up and slip them into my pocket for later. Her wet pussy glistens with her sweetness, and I can smell her arousal. I sit on the chair she was just on, slide forward, and suck on her clit. Wet and swollen, she whimpers as my tongue moves. Her head falls back as I slip a finger inside her tight hole. Dark hair is everywhere, her nipples are hard through her dress, and her breathing is labored.

My fingers and face were soaked with her juices. There's no hiding what we're doing, but I think that's only making her more turned on. She knows we can get caught at any second, and she loves the danger of it. Sure, we probably won't, but truthfully, there's no guarantee.

"I'm never going to be able to look at my desk the same." She whimpers.

I respond by pushing my finger in deeper. She bucks under my touch, and I smile against her clit. She's close, her body tightens as her breathing turns into pants. I want to watch her come undone. I slip in a second finger and feel her pulse against me. My tongue twirls across her clit, and she cries my name. It sounds like a primal scream.

"Zara!" If anyone is within in a mile radius, they definitely know what we were doing and who did what. But all I care about is the woman coming all over my face.

The second her orgasm finishes, Kim pulls me in for a kiss. Her tongue dips into my mouth, and she gets a taste of herself on my tongue. I moan as she presses her body against mine in a total frenzy. Is it possible she wants more?

"Can we go back to my place or yours? Somewhere we can both come as loud as we want?" Kim asks, panting lightly.

"Yes, Miss Stewart." I wink.

"If you keep that up, you'll end up under my desk again." She laughs.

"Wouldn't be the worst thing." I shrug.

Kim hops off the desk and fixes her dress. She starts looking for her panties, and I pull the pair from my front pocket and smile.

"May I have those back, please?"

"Nope. I think they're my souvenir."

Kim rolls her eyes to hide her smile as she gathers the rest of her stuff. I slap her ass playfully and grab a squeeze before unlocking the classroom door. I glance down the hallway to check if anyone's around, but it's still a ghost town. Not that I thought anyone would be randomly showing up now. I follow Kim to her car, and as she drives us back toward the Inn, I notice she's tense. Her phone keeps binging with texts, and each time, she grips the wheel a little tighter.

"Do you need to get that?" I ask casually.

"No."

"Is everything alright?" I tread lightly.

"Alana's texting me."

"And this is bad because?"

"I sort of yelled at her fiancé the other night after her bachelorette party."

"You what?!" I can't hide the shock in my voice.

"In my defense, he's an asshole."

"Okay, now I definitely need the whole story."

"Alana was wasted—like wasted, wasted. Which is fair, since it was her freaking bachelorette party. She was with friends, and we all kept an eye on her. Plus, she's a grown ass woman. Anyway, Will came to pick us up, and she puked on the hood of his car. So, of course he freaked out, and as soon as we got home, he dumped her on the bathroom floor and went to bed."

"What?!" I cut her off because I can't believe what she's saying.

"Yeah. He just went to bed. I thought he was getting something for her, or like, you know, coming back. But too much time passed, so I checked on her, and when I went to get her clothes, I sort of went off on him for being a bad fiancé. Then I told him that Alana deserves better than him." Kim winces while I'm in absolute awe of her.

"That's amazing."

"What?" Kim glances at me.

"I'm so glad you stood up to him. It seems like someone needed to. I wonder what Alana sees in him."

"I don't know. I was just so frustrated because it's one thing that he did that to me, and I have my own feelings about that, but to do that to the woman he's about to marry? It didn't sit right with me, and I had to say something."

"Well good for you; you should always speak your truth."

"But now every time she texts me, I'm anxious because we haven't spoken about it. He was gone the next morning, so when Alana woke up, I didn't tell her. I assume he told her, but I don't know what I'm supposed to say to her." She sighs.

"You tell her the truth. This is one of your oldest and best friends, right?" She nods. "Then you be honest about why you were upset and how he didn't take care of her. If she was as drunk as you were the night you saw me, it's possible she doesn't know that he left her."

"That's true."

"Either way, you should probably answer her because she's getting married in a few weeks, and you don't wanna give her more stress by ignoring her."

"You're right," Kim grumbles.

When we get to the Inn, Kim takes a few minutes to answer the texts from Alana. I head inside to see if Sandy is around for her walk. It's a little early, but I could take her down to the beach with Kim and she could get a little exercise in. I'm walking back out with Sandy when Kim sees us.

"All good?"

"Yeah, she just needed advice about something wedding related. I don't think Will told her anything," Kim explains.

"I mean, that can be a good thing, I guess? Maybe he didn't think it was worth mentioning to her?"

"I don't know. It sort of seems like he just doesn't care enough to tell her."

"Would you tell her?"

"This close to her wedding? I don't think so." She frowns. "Hi, Sandy! I was in my own world. How are you doing today, girl?"

Kim goes to bend down to pet her, but Sandy's nose goes right for her crotch, and I remember Kim's not wearing any panties. A look of pure horror flashes on her face as she realizes and quickly pushes Sandy away. Kim groans and I toss her the panties, letting her head inside to change before we take our walk. I don't need her accidentally flashing anyone on the beach. I'm more possessive than I should be, but I'm definitely not sharing her with anyone else.

"Come on, girl." Sandy and I walk along the path with Kim, the two of us are holding hands as Sandy walks between us.

Sandy gets disappointed when she doesn't see any kids on the beach. They usually give her snacks or have fun toys to play with. But not many people are around tonight. Kim relaxes under my touch, letting me keep holding her hand as we follow

Sandy around. We walk along the shore, following it until it ends just before the lighthouse. It's so beautiful this time of day, with the sun setting before us and the water breaking quietly. Kim's hair blows in the wind, and I shush that voice in my head that wants me to tell her how I feel.

TWENTY

Kim

Zara's sitting on my bed and finishing her rainbow eyeshadow while I try not to stare at her in the mirror. She's got her long blonde hair in bubble braids with cute rainbow butterfly clips. Her signature red lipstick is extra bright, and her face is shimmery from all the body glitter we used. But her outfit is what's going to make it hard to keep my hands to myself. She's wearing a rainbow crop top that's more like a bra, and her breasts are spilling out. She's paired it with black spandex shorts over a pair of fishnet tights. I have a rainbow crop top and matching shorts, leaving me feeling a tad underdressed.

"Do your friends go all out?" Zara asks.

"Oh, yes. One year, Heather dyed her hair rainbow colors. Another year, Ryleigh painted her body the bisexual pride colors." I laugh. It took her days to get that paint off.

"Isn't it weird that they're doing a pride event in August?"

"Sort of, but we're used to it. There are a lot of farmers markets and graduations, and when we used to have it in June, no one would go. So someone suggested moving it to August, and now every year it's a big event." I smile.

"That actually makes sense."

"I'm assuming you went to NYC pride?"

"Yep, every year since I was like, I don't know, fourteen? My older sisters used to take me, and then I eventually went with friends."

"I imagine it's quite different than this."

"Probably different in regard to size, but still just a super loving and welcoming event. I always feel so full of joy when I go." She smiles.

"That's why I like going."

"How are we getting there?"

"We're going to walk, if that's okay. The starting line for the parade is only ten minutes from here, and if we try to drive, there'd be absolutely no parking."

"Sounds good to me."

Zara puts on a pair of Converse with rainbow laces, and I grab my sneakers from the hall. I check my phone for any messages, but the last ones were from Heather and Ryleigh telling me to bring as much alcohol as I can fit in my purse. Zara and I have mini bottles of vodka and rum, along with a handful of cans of tall boys from the gas station. We grabbed whatever flavors they had and figured we'd wing it.

Norah, Gemma, and Alana aren't coming today. Alana has too much to do for the wedding, and Gemma is working, but Norah said she didn't feel up to it. I was worried she was sick or something, but she said it's just a little cold and nothing to worry about. Heather is bringing her new girlfriend, Sage, and Wrenn and Ryleigh are coming, too. I think Wrenn mentioned meeting up with her friends at some point, which I know Ryleigh is secretly worried about. I'm glad I have Zara coming with me—just in case my friends all go off on their own. This way, I won't be wandering around alone.

"Are those your friends?" Zara points to Heather, who's waving at me from afar the second we reach town.

"Yes." I wave back and take Zara's hand.

I think she's surprised, considering my usual no PDA rule, but it feels like today can be an exception. It isn't like anyone would be asking any questions at pride, it's a positive day of acceptance. I like the way her hand feels in mine, so I'm going to soak up as much of that as I can.

"Kim!" Heather wraps me in a hug, her sequin top poking into my chest. "This is my girlfriend, Sage. I think you guys have met, right?"

"We did." I laugh and say hi to Sage.

She's like the ultimate butch today, donning a snapback, a muscle tank top with a rainbow on it, and a pair of long shorts. Her neck is covered in rainbow lipstick kiss marks which I can tell Heather must've done.

"Hi, I'm Zara." She extends her hand to Heather and Sage.

"Oh, shit, yes. Sorry, this is Zara… she's my… Zara." I quickly save myself from saying something stupid. Everyone gives me the grace of ignoring the obvious and welcomes Zara to the group.

"Are Wrenn and Ry on their way?" I ask, looking around."

"They headed inside to grab drinks from the liquor store. I think they want something fancy." Heather shrugs. She's sipping a pink drink from a reusable coffee cup.

"It's about time! We getting lit, bitches!" Ryleigh's voice chants from behind us, and she dances her way over.

Her outfit puts everyone to shame—a pair of bright pink sequin pants, a purple tank top, and she dyed her hair blue for the day. She's a walking not-so-subtle bisexual pride flag. Wrenn tags behind her in a much more casual pansexual pride flag crop top and shorts that really can't be called shorts—they're that tiny. If Alana were here, she'd be freaking out at her little sister. That's probably why Wrenn wore them.

"Zara! So glad you made it!" Ryleigh pulls her in for a hug, and I forget—for a second—that they've already met.

"Good to see you again." Zara smiles.

"I heard the bakery is giving away free pot brownies," Wrenn tries to whisper, but she's clearly been drinking for a bit because her whisper is anything but.

"No way." Heather shakes her head.

"They want to try something new, hit a new base or something." Wrenn shrugs.

"If you lead my best friends to pot and there is none, you'll have to be buying them a dime bag or whatever it comes in these days." Ryleigh laughs.

"Fine, but I'm stopping by to see on the way through."

The parade is small, about ten floats from local businesses and clubs in town. They get some of the richer families and businesses to sponsor them and then have a group of kids from the schools decorate them. It's a nice tradition and it really brings the community together. I used to volunteer when I was a student, and now that I'm back, I'm sure I'll get a chance to help next year. There's a drag brunch at Teddy's afterward, and a bunch of family friendly events at the elementary school since they have the biggest space. The local businesses also do a pride scavenger hunt with things to do in each store.

I grab a Twisted Tea while she gets a Black Cherry Mike's Hard. We're not in the parade, but we aren't spectators either. We've found, over the years, that it's more fun to be behind the parade following in the joy along with the floats and the music. People dance and cheer along. It's very relaxed and better than slowly watching floats pass you by. The parade ends at the elementary school, after passing directly through town.

All my friends and their girlfriends are handsy with each other. Heather and Sage aren't as bad as Wrenn and Ryleigh—who are basically dry humping in front of everyone. I think this might be the first time we've all had girlfriends at the same time. I mean, Norah is still single, but everyone else is paired up. I think about Alana's wedding and how I have a plus one. I had told her I didn't need it anymore after Billy, but she had insisted

I keep it just in case I find someone. I don't know if it's the place or the vibe, maybe it's the Twisted Tea and the pot smoke I'm inhaling, but I blurt out the words to Zara before I can think.

"Will you be my date to Alana's wedding?"

Zara looks at me wide eyed. "When is it?"

Oh shit. My face falls. I hadn't even considered that. She's leaving soon. I don't know the exact day, because I haven't wanted to pop the bubble we're in.

"Labor Day weekend."

"I'm supposed to leave the last day of August." My face falls, but Zara catches my chin and tilts it toward her. "Let me check with Miss Taylor about staying extra, and I'd be happy to accompany you."

"Really?" I don't hide my excitement.

"Of course." She leans in to kiss me, and I swing my arms around her neck. I feel like I'm floating on air right now.

Zara tucks me under her arm, and we walk the rest of the parade together. I had crossed off so many things on my summer *fuck-it* list. Some of them I did without trying, and some I didn't even know I had. And it was all thanks to Zara. She pulled me out of my predictability and allowed me to be a new authentic version of myself. I still have all the pieces that I love while making room for the parts I want to change.

"I'm so freaking nervous. Wrenn wants me to meet all her friends but I'm afraid they'll hate me." Ryleigh pulls me aside to whisper in my ear.

"Why would they hate you?"

"I don't know how much Wrenn told them. If they knew about us hooking up in the past, then they might think I'm an asshole. And yeah, I used to be, but I'm not anymore."

"Maybe she didn't tell them anything. You didn't tell any of us about it," I point out.

"That's true." She nods.

"But if she *did* tell them, just show them you're not that person anymore. It was a while ago, and it's not like everyone stays the same. Just be yourself, and they'll see why Wrenn likes you so much."

"Thank you." She hugs me tightly. "You got a good one here, Z." Ryleigh winks at Zara.

"Don't I know it." Zara smiles back.

A knot forms in my stomach. There are only two weeks until the wedding. Two weeks until Zara leaves. I need to soak up every inch of that time—while not becoming a clingy girlfriend. I need to keep a balance while also not letting her know I'm going to be heartbroken when she leaves.

Yeah, not an issue at all.

Instead of freaking out about it like I want to, I push the knot away and promise to think about it later. Right now, I'm at pride with my best friends and the girl I like, and I want to enjoy this moment. I don't want to look back and realize I spent the entire day fixated on something I can't control anyway.

"You're so pretty," I tell Zara aloud. I don't think I tell her that enough, and I should.

"Oh, thank you. You're so pretty, too." Zara actually blushes. I definitely don't tell her this enough.

"No, I'm serious. Like, you have this amazing face, and god, those red lips. I'm in awe, really. Especially today. You look so hot. I just want to find a spot for us to go wild," I whisper the last part in her ear.

"Is your classroom open today?" she teases. Now I'm the one to heat up.

"We'd definitely get caught today!"

"Caught doing what?" Heather overhears.

"Uh, nothing." I blush.

"Did you guys do it someplace you shouldn't be?" Ryleigh joins in.

"ANYWAY. Look at how pretty the entrance to the school looks. They must've worked so hard on that," I say, trying to change the subject while Zara is laughing next to me.

"Who knew Kim had a wild side? You must bring that out in her." Ryleigh laughs.

"A *very* wild side." Zara winks at me, and I shake my head.

If those two gang up, I'll never get anywhere. I love that my best friend and the girl I like are getting along, but it's not going to end well if they start swapping stories.

TWENTY-ONE

Zara

When Kim told me she was ready for me to tie her up, I thought I was dreaming. I mean, I've been patient, and I didn't expect her to want me to yet. It's a big step, one that she hasn't taken before. I wasn't necessarily expecting her to come around and be so open to it. But for her to be excited about it, too?

"Do you have a safe word?" I look at her sitting on the bed patiently as I gather everything.

"Uh, I've never had one. Can it be anything?"

"Yeah, just something you'll remember and can say if you want to stop."

"Hmm, what about watermelon?"

"You're making a Harry Styles reference right now, aren't you?" I raise an eyebrow.

"Maybe." She laughs.

"Okay. Watermelon. Now, I can either tie your hands and feet to the bedposts—just your hands or feet. I can tie your hands behind you, or I can do some Shabari ties, if you'd like."

"What are Shabari ties?"

"Sort of like a fancy way to tie you up with rope where it

would be across your body, and you don't necessarily have to be stuck anywhere. It's more about the knots and feeling pleasure from them," I explain.

"Ah. Hmm." She thinks about it. "I think I want you to tie my hands behind me. You have the, uh, thing, right?"

"Are you referring to the strap on?" I ask, holding it up.

"Yes. I've never really used one before. My exes never wanted to." She blushes.

"I've been told it's similar to a dick, just harder." I shrug. "We don't have to use it, but it would be fun to have your hands behind you and fuck you from behind."

"Oh..." Her eyes light up.

"Yes?" I prompt her.

"I think I'd quite like that." She smiles.

"Sounds good to me."

I place the strap on the nightstand along with the robe and a pair of scissors.

"It's always important to have scissors nearby, just in case you want to be released immediately for any reason. I've never had to use them before, but I like to be cautious," I explain as her eyes dance across them.

"That makes sense. You've done a lot of..."

"Research. I've had partners I've used stuff with too, but I've taken classes so I can write about it informatively in my books."

Kim nods and I disrobe, letting it fall to the floor. Her eyes get big as the rake over the lingerie I'm wearing. Black and lace with a lot of cut outs to leave very little to the imagination. She bites on her bottom lip, and I smile.

"You look hot."

"Thanks." I climb on the bed and sit across from her.

"Anytime you wanna stop, say watermelon, okay? For a break or water or whatever."

"Okay."

I pull her legs across my lap and rest my hand on her thigh.

Kim's breath hitches as I lean in to kiss the side of her neck. Her hair falls back, and I bite down gently. She moans softly as I suck on her neck, her hands reaching for my breasts which are barely staying inside their top. As I bite down harder, she grabs my breasts harder and tugs on my nipple. I pull away, searching for her lips. She's wearing something shiny on her lips tonight, and as I lean in, I find it's some kind of cherry lip gloss. Sweet and not sticky like I anticipated. I groan into her mouth, and her tongue plays with mine.

She moves her legs, climbing on top of me, and we roll around the bed somewhat fighting for dominance. Our lips linger as our hands explore. When I climb on top of her, my legs locking her hips into place, I look at her under me, and she grumbles. She hates giving up dominance, but once she does, she's like a different person. Able to let go and orgasm bigger than I've ever seen. I rock my hips over hers, and I realize how dressed she is.

"We need you wearing less clothes. Now," I grumble against her skin.

I pull her T-shirt over her head, and I'm happily surprised to find she's not wearing a bra. Just two perky breasts and hardened nipples that meet my mouth.

"Yes, yes, yes." She whimpers quietly, tugging my head closer to her.

I use my free hands to reach between us and unbutton her shorts. I slip a hand past her lacey panties, and she moans, loudly.

"Oh, fuck!" she cries as I barely touch her pussy. My fingers dip down her center and feel how wet she is already.

"My girl is wet for me already? Someone must really want to be tied up…" I smirk. She groans as I take my fingers out of her, and I maintain eye contact as I lick them clean.

I slide my body down hers and move her shorts, then her panties, down her legs before tossing them across the room. Her bare pussy stares at me, and I can't resist taking a little taste. Kim grips the sheets as I suck gently on her clit.

"Oh, yes!" She cries, trying to get me to move. She grinds her hips into my face, but I refuse. I want to drag out her orgasm as long as possible.

"Please," she begs but I shake my head.

I flip her body over and grab her arms, holding them behind her back and reaching for the rope.

"You okay?"

"Yes." She's breathless but she wants this.

I take the rope and begin to loop it around her wrists, tying a knot to make sure she can't go anywhere. I leave a bit of slack for me to be able to pull her toward me while I'm fucking her. I make sure it's not too tight, and when she looks back at me, I can see her eyes deepening with desire. I smack her ass, watching it jiggle for me. I hit it twice more until I know she can't take it anymore. The anticipation is killing her.

I stand up to get the strap, sliding it on and then climbing back between her legs. She tries to look back at me but ultimately gives up with a groan. I tilt her hips toward me, helping her to lean on her knees. The sight of her hands bound does something primal to me. I knew how big this was to her and how much she must trust me to let me fuck her this way. I'm flattered; it means more than I could ever tell her.

I run my hand down her back, reaching where her hands are tied. Tugging on the rope, I pull her back toward me, so her ass is in the air and she's on her knees. I position myself between her legs and slip my hand between us to feel her. Gathering her juices on my fingers, I use them as lube for the strap.

"Mmm," she hums under me.

"Just like that, baby," I praise her as I slide the tip of the strap inside her.

She gasps as she feels how big it is compared to how tight she is. I go slow, not wanting to rush this and hurt her. I pull back her hair and tell her how good she's doing.

"You're doing great. Just a little more and I can fuck you so good," I whisper.

"Oh, Zara," she says breathlessly.

I fill her completely and move my hips slowly. She's tense, so I rub her back with one hand, and she relaxes. Then I move my hips more. This time letting my hips slam into her ass. Kim moans under me, and as I pull on the rope, she lets out a sultry moan.

"Fuck."

"I'm going to go faster, baby. Tell me if you can't handle it."

"I can handle it," she mutters before I even move.

So I move my hips and hold onto the rope, pulling her body toward me. I use my free hand to slap her ass, watching as my handprint appears in red. God, all of her ass would look so good this color. It's exactly like when she blushes for me. I pound into her, my hips bucking forward, and she cries out my name. She wants to move her hands. Her face is buried in the pillows as I plow into her.

"Fuck baby, just like that. You take me so good." I slap her ass again, and she clenches her hands into fists.

I reach around to grab her breasts, holding onto them while I fuck her. Her nipples are so sensitive, the second I brush against them, and she whimpers. She must be so close because she's panting under me.

"Are you close, baby?" She nods. "Do you want me to make you come?"

"Yes! Please!" she begs.

"Mmm, I suppose I can do that." I run my hand down her chest and stomach.

I stop to press just above her pubic bone, and she almost falls into the bed. So I reach farther down and rub slow circles on her clit. Thank god I'm ambidextrous; I have one hand on her clit while the other is on mine. I'm attempting to keep it slow, but the more I move my fingers on her the more I move on mine. It's a race I can't keep up with, so I don't try to. I'm a DJ, and her clit is my record—and fuck, with the way she sounds, everyone would love this music.

"Oh, yes!" It's me who cries out as I feel myself about to come.

"Fuuuuuck!" Kim cries under me.

Both of our orgasms hit at the same time. My fingers don't leave our clits, and my hips pound against her. Kim is panting on her knees, sweat glistening on her back, and we both collapse on the bed. I slide out of her slowly, and she leans over so I can untie her. My fingers are wet and a little numb from all the clit action, so it takes me a moment to untie her. But when I do, she stretches her wrists and lies with me.

"God, that was so fucking hot," she says.

I laugh because it's so like her.

"We are so doing that again," she says.

"Sounds good to me." I almost let the word *baby* slip off my tongue again. It's one of those things that's okay in the heat of the moment, but otherwise? Seems clingy.

"I think I saw literal stars during that last orgasm," Kim says in awe.

"Oh, yeah?"

"Yes. It was *that* good. Do you ever like being tied up?"

"Sometimes," I admit. "I'd let you tie me up if you wanted to try."

"Really?"

"Yeah, I trust you."

I say the words like they're no big deal. Like I've just said my favorite color—not that I'm willing to give her everything. She stays quiet as she thinks but pulls me closer. I can hear her heart beating just as fast as mine. The silent *thump-thumps* put my mind at ease. So I focus on those until my breath is even, and I don't feel so warm. Kim's quiet in a way that should make me nervous, but I know this is just her way of processing things. She'll talk again when she has something to say or to ask me. There's so much between us being left unsaid right now. I rub my thumb across the back of her hand over and over. She does the same, and every so often, she adds in a little squeeze as if to tell me she's still here. I wonder if I can commit this feeling to memory. If a few weeks from now, it would be nice to still feel the little squeezes and remember our time together.

TWENTY-TWO

Kim

"You really didn't have to pick me up," I tell Alana as I get into her car.

"I actually had ulterior motives for that, I hope it's okay. I brought you some coffee." She picks up an iced coffee and hands it to me.

I take it and sip it cautiously. It isn't like I thought she drugged me or something, but I'm confused about her motives.

"What's up?"

"So, Will and I had a talk about the night you stayed over. The night of my bachelorette party, and he mentioned that you yelled at him." Alana frowns.

"What?!" I'm so shocked, that I don't bother to contain it.

"He said it was nothing, but I thought we should talk about it. Him and I are about to be married, and I don't want there being any animosity between you and him—or me, by proxy."

"What exactly did he say I yelled at him about?"

"He said you were upset about that night he dropped you off with Zara. Which I completely understand, he and I had our own fight about that. You were drunk, under no circumstances should he have driven you there and not just home with us."

"I see." I'm trying to think of the best way to approach this.

"I just don't want you to be angry. You have every right to be upset, so is there anything I can do?"

"Truthfully, Alana, I did yell at him that night, and I did have an issue about that. But the bigger reason I yelled at him was because of how he treated you that night."

"What?" She looks surprised. I don't blame her. I'm sure she feels like this is coming out of nowhere.

"Do you remember anything from that night?"

"I remember the party, but after that it's sort of a blur. I know about throwing up on his car because he was not happy about that." She sighs.

"He brought the two of us home after Gemma and I carried you and laid you in the backseat. Then he just went to bed. He left you on the bathroom floor and didn't bother checking on you. I found you, took care of you, and went to get you pajamas. When I confronted him, I will admit, I was angry and heated. I yelled, which wasn't the best way to communicate. But he said you'd puke it off and be fine in the morning and didn't think his sleep should be interrupted because of you drinking so much. So yeah, I let him have it."

Alana's quiet as she mentally processes everything I'm saying. I'm silent, giving her a moment before I say anything else. I hope she believes me; we've been friends for almost two decades, but I've seen friendships end for worse reasons.

"He really left me there?" Her voice cracks, like she's on the verge of crying.

"He did. So yeah, I did yell at him. But I swear, Alana, it's only because I was so upset by how he was treating you." I reach for her hand and squeeze it gently.

"I-I didn't know. He made it seem like you just went off on him. Which didn't sound like you at all." She frowns.

"I told him that you deserved better than him, and I still think that's true."

"What? Do you just expect me to cancel my wedding or something?" She pulls back her hand.

"No! I just think you should talk to him. That's someone you're going to be spending your life with. I want to make sure it's someone who will take care of you in sickness, you know?"

"I know things with him haven't been perfect, or great lately. But we're usually not like this. We're usually happy and things work."

"I understand."

"It just feels like so much for this one day. I sort of can't wait for it to be over at this point," she says quietly.

"You don't have to marry him, you know."

"I want to," she says firmly.

I don't entirely believe her, but I also don't want to argue with her. She knows better than I do about what's best for her.

"We're going to be late for the nail appointment." She looks at the time, wipes the pending tears from her eyes, and starts driving toward the nail salon.

The rest of the drive is awkwardly silent. I can tell Alana's got a million things on her mind, and I don't want to add more than I already have. So I quietly sip the iced coffee and wait until we get there. All the girls, plus Gemma and Wrenn, are meeting us there to make sure we have matching nails for the wedding. Alana booked this months ago, and now the wedding is only a few days away.

Wrenn, Ryleigh, Heather, Norah, and Gemma are all waiting for us when we arrive. Norah's wearing a mask, which makes sense now that I know she's pregnant. It came as a complete shock to me, and it was a little unconventional, but I'm incredibly happy for her. I didn't know if she'd ever get the chance to be a mom, and she's definitely someone who should. She's been talking about having kids forever. It also makes sense that, although she doesn't need the mask to get her nails done, she's going to wear one anyway *just in case*. She's extra protective, and I respect that about her. She's going to do anything she can to protect that baby girl she's carrying.

"Hi, I have an appointment under Thomas. I want this for

everyone." Alana holds up a picture on her phone we can't see, and the woman at the front desk nods. She ushers everyone to the tables to do our nails. Our shoes are closed-toed, so at least we don't have to do pedicures today.

"What's up with Alana?" Norah whispers to me.

"It's complicated," I whisper back. I don't want to explain everything right now, and I know Norah won't push.

Alana takes a seat on the complete opposite side of me, and I'm sure it's going to be awkward for the rest of the day now. I know I probably shouldn't have said anything, but it's not like I could have kept my mouth shut about it when she's the one who brought it up. If she had never said anything about that night, I would have let it go. But now I'm the bad guy for standing up for my best friend.

I wish Zara were here right now. She's probably at the café not too far away, writing her book and listening to music. As the woman files my nails and my friends talk just out of earshot, I close my eyes. I think about Zara and how easy she makes everything.

"So, are you and Zara just pretending that she's not leaving after this weekend?" Ryleigh asks. Norah almost chokes on her water, and Heather hits Ryleigh's arm not so subtly. Had I been talking about her out loud or something?

"I never said that."

"So you guys have talked about it?" Ryleigh pushes.

"Well, no." I frown. I really didn't think I'd have to have this conversation here. I thought this was the one place I didn't have to think about it. What is with everyone cornering me today?

"Ryleigh, you don't have to push her on this," Norah says quietly.

"I'm just asking what she thinks is going to happen."

"I try not to think about it," I say truthfully.

"That's insane." Ryleigh huffs.

"Ryleigh!" Heather scolds aloud.

"She can't just put her head under a rock and pretend it's not happening. The girl she probably loves is leaving this weekend. How is she going to cope if she doesn't deal with it or at least tell her how she feels?"

"Babe, you've got to be kidding me. Talk about calling the kettle black or however the saying goes," Wrenn chimes in.

"What?" Ryleigh looks at her girlfriend in shock.

"You didn't tell me how you felt until very recently. And we've known each other for years. She just met this woman. Let her do her own thing," Wrenn adds.

"Fine." Ryleigh sighs. "I was just trying to help."

"I appreciate it. I just… I can't think about it. When I think about her leaving, everything hurts, and I just feel sad."

"Some would take that as a sign to tell her how you feel. Maybe not you, but some." Ryleigh tries to be casual, but Heather is rolling her eyes.

"I need some air." I stand up, excusing myself and stepping outside.

My nails are only half done, but I can't handle this right now. I know Ryleigh's right, but that's not the point. I don't want to tell Zara how I feel because I know it won't change anything. She has an entire life I don't even know about back in New York. An apartment, a daily routine, friends—and I don't fit into that. I live here with my new job that I'm excited about. We're not just going to change jobs and move for some person we just met. No matter how I feel about her.

"Hey, you okay?" Heather comes out and sits next to me on the bench.

"Yeah, I just needed a second."

"You know Ryleigh comes from a place of love."

"I do. I just don't feel like placating her right now."

"That's fair. She gets a little stubborn, but she has your best interest at heart."

"What do you think?" She looks at me, confused. "About Zara and me?"

"Oh!" Heather hesitates. "Well, I like her, and I like her for you. I think if she lived here or you had any intention of moving, it would be a great fit. But in reality, neither of you probably wants that and don't know much about how the other lives. Flings can be fun, but it's hard when you have to let it run its course."

"So you think it might be the end?"

"I honestly don't know. I mean, Ryleigh is right—you should talk to her either way. But it really depends on how you both feel and how much the other is willing to give."

I nod, and we head back inside. We can't keep the nail artists waiting on us all day. So I slip back into my chair and try to join in the rest of the conversations. Alana still isn't looking at me, Ryleigh is arguing with Wrenn about something, while Norah and Gemma try to stay out of it. I'm starting to realize how stressful this weekend is going to be.

At least Zara will be joining us for most of it. She picked out a bunch of fancy dresses online, letting me choose which one I thought would go best. She doesn't want to accidentally look like a bridesmaid or something. We have a few nights planned at her room in the Inn, realizing it's more fun to be loud there. Plus, there's the added bonus of seeing Sandy.

She got to extend her stay, so she's leaving Monday morning after the wedding. I don't know the specifics because I don't want to. It's silly, but if I don't know them, I can still pretend it's not happening. I'm living under a rock. But a very well-taken-care-of rock that's keeping a lot of things stable right now.

Once the wedding is over, I can unpack the whole thing. Zara and my summer fling, the summer fuck-it list, everything. But for now, I'm on bridesmaid duty, making sure this wedding goes off without a hitch. Even if I think the groom is an asshole.

TWENTY-THREE

Zara

"Well, finally! I swear I haven't heard from you all summer!" Haley says on the other end.

"We literally talked a few days ago." I shake my head. She is so dramatic.

"Fine, fine, sue me for missing my best friend. Are you excited to be coming back home?"

"Yeah," I say, but my heart isn't fully in it. I'm toying with the photos Kim left on my desk from Pride—me, her, and all her friends decorated to the nines with smiles on our faces.

"That doesn't sound like someone excited to come back to the greatest city on earth," she teases.

"I am."

"But?" she prompts.

"I—I met someone," I say quietly. But the shriek I hear from the other end is deafening. I hold the phone away from my ear until I hear her quiet down.

"Tell me everything! I knew you'd find someone. I just had this gut feeling. Oh my goodness, it's why your pages have been so good, right? You found yourself a muse."

"She's not just a muse." I don't know why I feel the need to defend her. It's not a bad thing to be someone's muse—it's just more than that.

"Oh? Tell me more."

"We met at the beginning of the summer, and it was going to be a one-time thing, but we hit it off. So now we've had a summer fling. Except I think it could be more. But neither of us has really broached that subject, so I don't know." I sigh.

"You're so bad for this chick."

"I am not!" But I know that I am.

"Sure. So you haven't mentioned her all summer because?"

"I was annoyed you were right, and I didn't want it to end."

"Well, who says it has to end?"

"No one survives long distance, and I live in New York with you. She lives here—she's a kindergarten teacher, for Christ's sake."

"That's so adorable, I love it."

"I'm serious, Hales."

"I am too. Why doesn't long distance work? It's a few states away, and it's not like we don't live in the age of cell phones and FaceTime. Plus, you're freelance, so why can't you take weekend trips to see her or have her fly to you for school breaks?"

"Well…" I frown. I haven't really thought that far ahead, I guess.

"If you want it to end with her, sure, end it. If it was just a summer fling, then pack your bags and come home. But if you're extending your trip for her, writing effortlessly for the first time in ages, and feeling sad about leaving her, then maybe take the time to at least talk to her about whether leaving is the right thing to do."

"You might be right."

"I'm always right. You just rarely listen to me." Haley laughs.

"Oh, fine."

"You just seem… happy. Not that you aren't usually happy, but I've never heard you talk about someone else with this much ease. You seem scared to let it go. So maybe see what happens if you try to hold on a little longer."

"What if that's not what she wants?"

"Well, at least you'll know you tried. But if she spent all summer with you and is as happy as you sound, then she might be feeling the same."

"Maybe you're right."

"I'm always right. Can we get brunch when you're back in town? I've been bored out of my mind all summer."

"Of course. Unlimited mimosas are calling my name." I smile.

We say goodbye, and I lean back in my chair to think. I was only supposed to come up with a few ideas for my next series, but instead, I came back with an entire series plotted and one full book written. Sure, it's a rough draft—emphasis on rough—but it's also my first completed manuscript in that short amount of time. Haley is right; the words just flew out of me, and I know why. Kim makes me feel free and happy. She brings out this other side of me that I didn't even know was dormant. She allows me to have fun and be a new person while she breaks free of her shell.

I'm not ready to say goodbye, and I know my heart isn't either. I've been dreading this for the last few weeks, and when she asked me to stay for Alana's wedding, I was so grateful I had a reason to delay going. An extra three days where anything could happen. I'll get to see her bridesmaid's dress and watch her friend marry a shitty guy. I'll get to watch her catch the bouquet and taste her with her legs wrapped around my head. It would be the perfect way to end us.

But maybe it could be the perfect way to ask her to give us a shot.

Kim said the weekend kicks off on Friday night with the rehearsal dinner, followed by the wedding on Saturday and the wedding party brunch on Sunday. She is jam-packed all weekend with things to do but assured me I'm invited to it all.

She also mentioned it would be super boring but that I'd make it a lot more fun if I came. I've been to enough of my sisters' weddings to know how boring and crazy they can be, but I don't mind roughing it for her. If she feels relaxed with me being there, then I'll be there.

It's all taking place at a hotel in the next town over, which isn't far, so no one is spending the night or anything—but maybe Kim and I will. I could surprise her with a reservation, hotel room sex, and all the romantic things I was too afraid to do this summer. Then, maybe at the end of the weekend, I could tell her how I feel and see if she wants to try long distance. I know it won't be easy, but I think it would be worth it.

I already let Miss Taylor know I won't be around this weekend to walk Sandy but will make sure to say goodbye before I leave. That dog really grew on me, and I'm going to miss our daily walks. I'm leaving my stuff in the suite since I'm technically staying here until my flight. I haven't actually booked it yet, but I will. I know I have to. I've put off leaving for as long as I possibly can. It doesn't make sense to be paying rent on an apartment I'm not even living in.

I pull out my laptop and get to work on making this happen. I reserve the second-best suite in the hotel and make sure they fill it with champagne and flowers. I've been packing my stuff little by little for the last week. I have one full suitcase of dirty clothes, and the rest I've been organizing. I pack a bag for this weekend, full of my makeup, hair supplies, and the dresses I'll need. I just have to figure out a way to make sure Kim brings all her stuff to the hotel so we won't have to come back to town until Monday.

TWENTY-FOUR

Kim

Zara and I get ready for the rehearsal dinner together. I have a strapless, light green dress, and she has on a dark green, almost black one. She looks elegant with her hair pulled back into a low bun while I curl mine. I'm nervous. This is our last weekend together, and we're spending it at a wedding I don't want to be going to. Not that I can say that out loud. But Alana has barely spoken to me, and I definitely don't support this marriage. I can see who she is turning into, and it makes me sad. She has lost so much of herself, and she barely notices it. It's hard when the line between doing what is right and being a good friend is on opposite sides.

"You look beautiful," Zara murmurs in my ear.

"Thank you." I lean into her lips, letting them graze my cheek.

"Mmm, you smell good too." She takes a deep inhale and breathes in my perfume.

"If you keep looking at me like that, we're going to be late," I warn her.

"So?" She smirks at me.

"You know I can't be late." I sigh, pushing her body away so I can grab my heels.

"Okay, you're right. But later, you're all mine." She winks.

Zara has convinced me to stay with her this weekend. I have my bag packed with everything I need so I won't need to come back to my apartment at all. She is insistent that we deserve a weekend together. Not that I'm not impressed by the Inn, but we've spent so many nights there already—I don't know what makes this weekend special. Except for the fact that it's our last one.

Zara and I piled everything into the car earlier, not wanting to mess up our hair and makeup once it's done. Now that we look ready, I grab my keys and lock up my apartment behind us. I drive us to the hotel where the wedding is. The rehearsal dinner is taking place in one of the banquet halls. It's sort of unnecessary, but Alana's family is insistent on having one to make sure everyone knows their place. I'm just glad Zara is coming with me. I'm not looking forward to the start of this weekend, which I guess is obvious by the way my leg is shaking since Zara holds it still with her hand.

"Sorry, just a lot of nerves."

"Do you want to talk about it?"

I shrug instead of answering. It's a cop-out, but I don't know how to tell her that I don't want her to go. I don't know how to tell my best friend she deserves better than the man she's marrying, and I definitely don't know how to act normal this weekend. So I don't say anything. Zara puts on a Harry Styles playlist, and as he sings, I relax. I hum along to the words, and I can feel the stress easing. His melodic voice and Zara beside me are all I need to get through the weekend.

When we pull up to the hotel, we're immediately escorted inside with help for all our stuff. There's a valet for my car, and I follow Zara inside. I'm looking around for my friends when Zara excuses herself to ask the concierge a question. When she returns, I still don't know where my friends are, but she looks like she has good news.

"So, I have a surprise for you." She holds up a gold key card.

"You got a room?"

"I got us a room." Zara holds out her hand, and I take it suspiciously.

I follow her to the elevator, and she presses the button for the suites. She didn't just get us a room—she got us an insanely expensive and romantic one. Down the hall from the elevator, she unlocks the door and lets me in first. The bellhop has already dropped off our bags, but my eyes go toward the bucket of champagne and the bouquet of roses on the bed. Had she done all this?

"I thought we could enjoy our last weekend together. I know we should probably talk about things, but for now, I just wanted to enjoy these last few nights together. And you deserve all this and more." She smiles. My eyes water as I look around the room and back at her.

Instead of speaking, I wrap my arms around her and hold her body close. She kisses me slowly, delicately. Like she's afraid to break me. A few loose tears slip from my cheeks, but she catches them each time. I don't know how to say the words I feel. Thankfully, with Zara, I know I don't have to. She knows what I'm feeling and how I feel without me saying a word.

"Let's go find your friends." She takes my hand, and I glance in the mirror by the door before leaving. Thank god for waterproof mascara.

Everyone is waiting in the lobby when we return. Apparently, we are the first ones here. Alana and Will are off somewhere setting up for the rehearsal, but all the bridal and groom parties are here, along with Will and Alana's immediate family. I make a beeline for my girls, hoping I can tune out everyone else.

"Is everyone here?" Heather asks, looking around.

"I think Will's family is over there." Gemma nods toward the group of gorgeous-looking people gathered on their phones. They haven't spoken a word or looked up at anyone else. Yup, definitely seems like his family.

"Have they talked to anyone?" Norah frowns.

"Nope. They checked in at the front desk and have been sitting there quietly. My parents tried talking to them, and they gave one-word answers. My mother is pissed." Wrenn nods toward the other side of the lobby, where her mom is fuming.

"You'd think they'd be happy their son is getting married." Heather sighs.

I look around the lobby and see Alana and Will walking over. He's got his phone glued to his hand, and she looks happy to see us but not thrilled to be next to him. I don't think that's how two people about to be married should look. They split, Alana joining our group and Will greeting his family. They all drop their devices and hug him as he escorts them toward the rehearsal dinner room. Alana does the same, and I try to zone out while listening for my name. Zara takes my purse and a seat in the guest section while Alana goes over who is matched with who and when to walk. They don't have a ring bearer or flower girl since they don't have any young children in the family, so it's mostly us. I have to walk with Will's old college roommate, whose name might be Chad or Brad. I'm not really listening. He introduces himself, and he seems nice enough.

We go through the motions of the wedding twice before Alana and Will excuse themselves to talk. Although "talk" is a strong word when we can hear them yelling at each other down the hallway. I know tensions are high and things seem to be off, but it feels like this goes past wedding jitters. Zara and I catch each other's eye to have a silent conversation. I want to know if I should say anything, but we both think it's best that I don't.

After they come back and we rehearse a few more times, we have the actual dinner. Lots of wine is passed around, and there's a ton of food to choose from. Alana makes sure there is a special plate for me and even hand-delivers it so I know it's safe to eat. It's the first positive interaction we've had, and it lasts for all of three seconds. By the end of the night, I'm relieved to have an excuse to head to bed. Not that I'm tired, but I'm ready to not be in these heels or plastering a fake smile on my face.

"God, I can't wait to get you out of this dress," Zara mutters the second we're alone in the elevator.

I press her back against the wall and kiss her fiercely.

"I want you so bad," I admit.

The doors open, and the second we're back in the room, I throw off my dress. I think Zara and I are on the same page until I turn around and see her pouring us each a glass of champagne.

"I thought maybe we could have a glass and talk a little before we fall into bed?"

"Oh, sure." I look for a shirt in my bag that I can toss over my panties and then sit on the bed.

Zara sits across from me and hands me the glass. I smile, take a small sip, and then look at her expectantly.

"So, I think we both had different expectations at the beginning of the summer. What started as a one-time thing slowly transformed into friends with benefits. I had an amazing summer with you, and I wouldn't change a thing about it. I have enough memories to last a lifetime with you." Zara takes a deep breath.

Here it comes.

She's about to break things off before the weekend was even starting.

"I was wondering if you'd want to make more?"

"What?" I look at her, confused.

"I know it's not for everyone, but I thought maybe we could try long distance. I could come up some weekends, you could join me in New York on school breaks. We have FaceTime and social media and texting. I know it's a long shot, and if this isn't something you want, that's okay. But I don't feel like I could go back to New York without even asking if it's a possibility to be with you."

"You want to try long-distance friends with benefits?"

Zara lets out a laugh. "No, you silly, beautiful woman. I want to try being your long-distance girlfriend."

"Oh." My mouth forms a tiny *O* as I try to think about this.

I hadn't expected this even being an option. But it makes sense. We're grownups, and there are a million ways to keep in contact these days. We want more time to get to know each other without just up and leaving our lives behind. It's actually extremely smart and well thought out. I don't know why I'm surprised.

"You don't have to say yes."

"No!" Zara's face falls. "I mean, yes! Like, no I'm not saying no. I'm saying yes. I'd love to be your girlfriend. I just didn't think you'd even want to do that. I'm not ready for a big step, but this makes sense for us. I'd love more time getting to know you because what I've seen so far, I've loved," I admit.

Zara relaxes, takes the glass from my hand to put it on the nightstand, and then kisses me. I don't know how long our lips stay together, but it's long enough that I need to ask for air. We're all giggles and body parts as she touches me. She melts against me as we clink teeth, smiling. We climb under the satin sheets, and she explores my body like it's the first time. I know it might not be forever, but in this moment, I know how much I like Zara. I have a feeling stronger than hope…maybe this really will work. All because I used this summer to become a little less predictable and say yes a little more.

Zara is the best thing I've ever said yes to.

BONUS EPILOGUE

KIM

Zara holds my hand as I make the turn into the airport. There's too many cars coming and going to be able to tell where we're supposed to be. So I rely on the GPS and the signs to get me to the parking lot so I can walk her in. I wish it was simpler, like back when you could walk the person all the way to their gate and watch their plane take off. But I guess it's safer this way. As I turn into the parking lot, I know I'm about to pay at least twenty bucks for a five minute goodbye but I wasn't ready to do a quick drop off. We both knew we were holding off the inevitable.

After Alana's failed wedding, I knew I needed to stay in town for her. So instead of visiting New York with Zara right away, I'd be there to visit in a few weeks. It sucked, but I knew Alana was going to need me more right now. Even though no one knew where she was for 48 hours. When we finally located her, it was like a sigh of relief on everyone.

"Ready?" I look at Zara as I turn off the car and put my phone in my pocket.

"Yeah." She nods.

I help her get her suitcases out of her trunk and we both wheel one toward the airport entrance. We hold hands as we cross the busy road at the crosswalks and then stop inside. We move to the side so no one gives us a hard time about being in the way.

"We can make this work." I don't know if she's saying it to me or as a reminder to herself.

"We can." I nod. Suddenly I can feel tears falling from my cheeks. I can't stop them and I wasn't prepared for them either.

"Hey, it's going to be okay. We can do this." Zara pulls me in for a hug. I try not to, but I end up sobbing into her t-shirt as she rubs my back.

"I-I...just...miss...you..." My words come out incoherently.

"I'm going to miss you too." She whispers softly.

I try to commit this moment to memory. How her t-shirt smells, how she looks at me and the way she holds me. It's this feeling that's going to get me though the next few weeks until I can see her again.

"I'll text you as soon as I land, and we can facetime later. I know you're busy and you'll be checking up on Alana but we'll find time." She assures me.

"I can't believe she didn't get married."

"I know, but I think you sort of called it too. You knew she was too good for Will, it was just good she finally realized it herself."

"I really loved getting to know you this summer." I whisper, as I wipe my eyes.

"I loved it too." She holds my face in her hands and smiles at me. Her red lipstick perfectly in tact, her blue eyes staring back at me.

"I...I love you." I wince, afraid of what she might say back.

"I love you too." She breathes me in just long enough for me to relax before kissing me.

Her red lips melt into mine while I breathe in her minty fresh breath. She calms as I wrap my hands around her neck and she tugs me in tighter by the waist. My heart rate increases as I fall into her. I forget we're in a crowded airport, that anyone is even around us. I just care about saying goodbye to the woman I love. When I pull back, we're both crying. Tears flying from our eyes and we look at each other and laugh. We can't help it.

"I didn't think I'd be crying but suddenly I'm realizing how much I'm going to miss you. Like I knew it was a lot, but actually leaving you is making this ten times harder." Zara says quietly.

"We should've brought tissues. I feel so underprepared." I tease.

"Thank you for making this summer unimaginable. I loved getting to know you and falling more and more for you."

"I did too. I'm going to miss being able to drive five minutes away to see you." I sigh.

"Well you'll still have to go see Sandy and Miss Taylor right?"

"Of course." I nod. She had sort of roped me into taking Sandy on nightly walks now that Zara was headed home. I didn't mind it, I was a dog person and I knew Miss Taylor needed the company. I just also knew I'd be missing Zara even more if I was going to be there every night.

"I should go, I have to check in my bags and find my gate."

"Okay. Plus you probably want to get some writing done too?" I guess.

"You're right. The airport really is the best place to get work done though. I'll probably order a cocktail since I'm all out of my gummies." Zara laughs.

"Just don't drink too many and miss your flight. Actually, maybe that isn't a bad idea."

Zara smiles and replies by kissing me again. This time slower and with more intention. She's saying goodbye. Not the goodbye where I should be worried I'll never see her again, but the goodbye kiss to hold me over until we see each other again. Zara is the one to pull away this time and I wipe her tears away with my hand. I hold my hand there just for a moment and then step back. She takes her bags in her hands and does a deep sigh.

"I'll see you soon, okay?"

"Okay." I nod.

It hurts, but I watch as she strolls across the airport to the self check in and begins the process of leaving. I'm stuck on the outside watching her. I can't go any further without a ticket and I don't want to stand here like some kind of stalker. She waves one last time and I blow her a kiss back. Then I start walking toward the car. Of course by the time I get there, I'm crying even harder than before. My mascara is running and I look scary, but I didn't care. The only person I wanted to impress was about to get on a plane.

As I slide into my car I notice a note sticking out of the book I was reading. Zara's latest book. Not the one she wrote this summer but the one she had published in May. It was a stand-alone thankfully so I picked it up last week. I was too curious not to read what she had written. Of course the moment she saw me reading it she had freaked out and told me not to read it in front of her. I'd never seen her so embarrassed before. It was adorable.

I slide the note out of the book and my name is scrawled across the front.

Kim,

By the time you're reading this I'll probably be on the plane or somewhere without any service. I wanted to tell you this in person but I wasn't sure I'd have the guts before I left. I guess this is easier since you don't have to say it back right away. Maybe you find this letter days from now. Although I have a feeling you might notice this note right away.

Anyway, I love you Kim. I've never fallen so hard for someone and I can't see myself ever falling so hard again. I am scared about what the future holds but I'm also excited. I never anticipated being with you and now that I have you, I can't remember life before you. God, this is so cheesy. If I put this in a romance book my readers would tell me this was too cheesy. But I guess that's how it is to be in love.

I hope to see you soon.

Yours,
Zara

By the time I'm done reading, my eyes are overflowing with tears again. I hold the letter close to my chest and reread it over and over. I wanted to remember this. She was going to tell me she loved me, even if I didn't say it. She didn't say it back because I said it first, she said it back because she truly felt the same. I relax a little knowing just how much she cares for me. Then I open my phone, turn on a countdown app for when I'll see her again and hope the time doesn't pass by too slowly.

Also by Shannon O'Connor

SEASONS OF SEASIDE SERIES

(each book can be read as a standalone)

Only for the Summer

Only for Convenience

Only for the Holidays

Only to Save You

Seasons of Seaside: The Complete Collection

LIGHTHOUSE LOVERS

Tour of Love

Hate to Love You

To Be Loved

Inn Love

Love, Unexpected

BEHIND THE SCENES SERIES

Eras of Us

Not My Fault

ETERNAL PORT VALLEY SERIES

Unexpected Departure

Unexpected Days

Eternal Port Valley: The Complete Collection

STANDALONES

Electric Love

Butterflies in Paris

All's Fair in Love & Vegas

Fumbling into You

Doll Face

Poolside Love

THE HOLIDAYS WITH YOU

(each book can be read as a standalone)

I Saw Mommy Kissing the Nanny

Lucky to be Yours

The Only Reason

Ugly Sweater Christmas

EVERGREEN VALLEY SERIES

How the B*tch Stole Christmas

POETRY

For Always

Holding on to Nothing

Say it Everyday

Midnights in a Mustang

Five More Minutes

When Lust Was Enough

Isolation

All of Me

Lost Moments

Cosmic

Goodbye Lovers

About the Author

Shannon O'Connor is a twenty something, bisexual, self published author of several poetry books and counting. She released her debut contemporary romance novel, *Electric Love* in 2021. O'Connor is continuously working on new poetry projects, book reviews, and more, while also diving into motherhood. When she's not reading or writing she can be found watching Disney movies with her son where they reside in New York. She is currently a full time mom and full time author.

She sometimes writes as S O'Connor for MF romances and as Shannon Renee for Poly romances.

Heat. Heart. & HEA's.

Check out more work & updates on:
Facebook Group: https://www.facebook.com/groups/shanssquad

Website: https://shanoconnor.com

- facebook.com/AuthorShanOConnor
- instagram.com/authorshannonoconnor
- bookbub.com/authors/shannon-o-connor
- pinterest.com/Shannonoconnor1498
- threads.net/@authorshannonoconnor

Printed in Great Britain
by Amazon